IZZY ORTS

A NOVEL

G.E. WILCOX

Dedicated to my wife Sandra.

Chapter 1

The forest was quiet and peaceful, birds were lazy in the afternoon's warmth and dozed on their perches as time merged between past and future and the present seemed unreal. If there was a war, a conflict raging, it was not here, not at this moment. The forest was tranquil and harmonious among the sighing trees and wisps of converging scents.

Private Boyce sat astride a fallen branch, his back supported by the main trunk. His shaven head glistened with sweat, accentuating the white, furrowed scar running across his crown from front to back, the result of an altercation with a drunken Polish sailor.

He busied himself, scraping the last deposits of dried blood from the carefully honed edge of his hunting knife.

Smearing oil on both sides of the blade, he polished the hardened steel to a mirror finish and examined his amorphous image in the convex blade, a grotesque, thin grizzled head with five black holes reflected back at him, he grinned and slid the knife back into its sheath.

Boyce made a small slingshot from a rubber band and flexed it between his two middle fingers. On the periphery of his vision he spotted a likely target and keeping still he waited until the butterfly had alighted on the head of a dandelion, before slowly raising his right hand, two fingers forming a 'V', braced against the tension of a rubber band. The thick rubber band constricted around the acorn projectile as Boyce pulled the lazzy band back. Drawing a bead on the resting insect, Boyce raised his aim slightly to compensate for trajectory and made slight adjustments before firing the acorn at the unsuspecting insect. The nut arced through the air slicing the stem of the dandelion in two, and as the head fell away the graceful butterfly bobbed away on the gentle breeze.

Boyce cursed to himself and reloaded. Bored, he wiped the filthy sweat from his filthy head with his filthy vest and lit a bisected Woodbine.

He found the forest oppressive, and longed for the hustle, the smell and vibrancy of the overcrowded streets of London. He hated trees and the overbearing sultry silence and the nasty little insects that inhabited the place. They had a tendency to crawl into his nooks and crannies during the night and wake him screaming and cursing.

2

Boyce lit and sucked on his flattened half cigarette and cursed his luck. He picked some loose tobacco off his tongue and examined it before flicking it away. Looking over his shoulder, he peered across the clearing at Simms, who was playing with his beloved radio, black Bakelite earphones clamped to his bony head.

Simms was sitting under a sycamore, concentrating on his big tuning dial. He peered at life through round metal-rimmed spectacles that hooked around his red, protruding ears. His thin, naked torso emerged from his ill-fitting khaki trousers like a toadstool growing from a tree stump. Occasionally, he would wave his arms in the air to ward off irritating bugs that would constantly hover around him, waiting for their chance to nip in and take a bite.

Boyce sent off another acorn targeted at Simms's sweating head, but falling short, it ricocheted off his steel helmet, which was lying on the grass beside him, and caught Simms across his left cheek with enough velocity to draw blood. Simms flinched at the sudden pain and, snatching off his headphones, he felt his sore cheek as he stood up. His first instinct was that one of his tormentors had bitten him, until he looked over at Boyce, who was smirking and pretending it was nothing to do with him.

'You toe rag, Boyce. Why don't you grow up?'

'Ere, I don't know what you're talking about.'

'Cockney cunt.'

'Flapper.'

Simms spat on his fingers and smeared saliva on his cheek, 'if you damage this radio transmitter, the corporal will 'av your guts.' 'I don't think so.' Boyce shouted back in a sarcastic tone. He winked and gave Simms two fingers.

'You thick bastard' said Simms, who regretted saying the words out loud as soon as he had said them, bracing himself for the axiomatic consequences of calling Boyce 'thick' or a 'bastard', especially in the same sentence.

Boyce's face had turned from one of candour to hostility, from pasty white to a fleshy red. After the initial hiatus, as his brain slowly digested the insult, he sprang to his feet and charged across the open ground. Simms, who had been expecting the reaction, had already distanced himself and was heading for a large oak tree to take refuge. Boyce ran after him, wailing and ranting insults.

The two young soldiers circled the massive trunk, going one way and then the other, Boyce cursing and chasing Simms around the ancient tree, threatening to cut things off his body and ram them into certain orifices. Boyce screamed so much that his voice croaked into a high-pitched falsetto that bounced and echoed around the glade, setting off flurries of wings as birds left their perches for safety.

Simms tried vying for time. 'I'm sorry Boyce, I didn't mean it, for Christ's sake.' 'I'm going to cut your balls off.'

'Calm down now, I said, I'm sorry.' Simms kept looking behind him for an escape route.

Boyce crept around the Oak towards the sound of Simms's voice, looking at the ground for any tell-tale shadow. Simms, sensing his approach, stepped over the huge roots, away from Boyce.

'Let's call a truce,' said Simms. 'it's too hot to muck about.'

They continued circling the tree like Mayday revellers as Simms waited for Boyce to answer.

'You call me stupid once more and I'll ram this knife up your jacksie.' Boyce said, half heartedly.

'Sorry me 'old mucker,' Simms grinned, as he knew Boyce was starting to give in.

Boyce walked away from the old Oak, mumbling to himself. He turned as Simms appeared and shouted back, 'Your turn to make tea, Simmo.'

'You're not going to cut my balls off, then?' Boyce waved his newly oiled knife in the air, before replying, 'No. just your ears till your spec's fall off,' Boyce laughed at his own joke.

'We have a truce then, an understanding?' 'What?'

'I said I'm sorry for implying that you are a cretin.'

'A wot?'

'A cretin. It's er, Latin for genius.' Simms replied, studying Boyce's face carefully to see if he swallowed it.

As Boyce thought about it, Simms, anticipating some sort of treachery, slopped off and lost himself among the trees, allowing Boyce time to cool down. He strolled off down a track past a wrecked lorry, its back axle and wheels blown off by a landmine and lay some yards from the vehicle. The contents of the lorry lay strewn around the glade, broken boxes, ammunition, jerry cans and medical supplies. White bandages had unrolled across the ground amid clusters of shell dressings and kidney-shaped white enamel containers with blue edging. But the most important part was the small wooden boxes with a red cross on the side. These contained various ointments, pills, and morphine syrettes.

Luckily, the upward blast of the mine had ripped through the rear flatbed of the lorry and left the side mounted petrol tank undamaged or the whole thing would have gone up in one huge, fireball.

He carried on down the single dirt track, keeping to the centre to avoid the two parallel ruts carved out of the ground by carts and other wheeled vehicles over time. He knew also that there could be some more mines in the area.

Simms stopped in front of three graves dug into the verge and bearing three hastily made wooden crosses, the cross pieces made from a section of packing case, tied at the centre with rope. Carved across the centre of the middle cross was an inscription that read, *'Deus Vobiscum.'* He wondered what that meant as he pushed his specs back up the bridge of his sweating nose and peered into the dense mass of foliage, hearing the rustle and scratching of the foraging birds and small mammals that put nerves on edge.

All along the side of the road, the green verge was peppered with different hues of white to grey stumps of cut trees, vainly pushing out fresh shoots to compete for the diffused light. The air felt warm, sticky, and congealed. He wiped the trickle of sweat from his cheek, wincing as he pressed the purple blue bruise. The squirrel gymnasts busied themselves overhead, springing from tree to tree, chattering and arguing the toss.

Leaving the graves, he wandered down the track, scanning the bend ahead for any sign of the corporal and the rest of the troop. The track ahead was empty save for a few leverets playing among the pools of speckled sunlight. An unusual cooling breeze came upon him and he closed his eyes, breathing in hard through his nose, sucking the cool air into his lungs and finding a quiet spot behind a clump of ferns he sat down a lit a cigarette.

With no sign of the others returning, he walked back to the glade, avoiding eye contact with Boyce. His previous tantrum now dissipated and was now occupying himself by prizing the petrol cap off the wrecked lorry. Simms continued his monitoring work with the radio transmitter which, was now only a receiver as the transmitter valve had broken. He sat down next to a fallen tree trunk and, keeping tabs on Boyce, donned his earphones. As the crackle and hiss of static seeped through his head, he watched as Boyce fed a black rubber hose down the neck of the petrol tank. He sucked, his cheeks hollowing as his lungs expanded.

Simms waited for the inevitable as Boyce exploded, spitting copious amounts of the volatile fluid out of his rubber mouth and down the front of his trousers. He kept his thumb over the end of the black tube as he vomited and, wiping the crud from his mouth, he filled an old biscuit tin with petrol. Boyce, a stupid grin on his face, winked at Simms when he noticed he was being observed. 'How about that brew up then, Simmo?' Boyce said, mouthing the words as Simms had his phones on before lifting the tin and carrying it carefully back to his fallen branch.

Simms sighed and, removing his earphones, went to retrieve the paraffin stove. Anything to keep the peace until the corporal gets back, he thought.

'I'll put the kettle on. You sit and rest awhile,' said Simms, feeling a little parched himself.

'Can't stand this 'angin about Simmo, bloody hell. Two sugars in mine.'

'You'll be lucky.'

'Wot, I can't stand tea without sugar in it.' Boyce sneered.

'I'll send the Butler out to procure some supplies sir.' muttered Simms. He turned his attention to the tea and pumped the primus with vigour, topped off the alloy kettle and set it on the stove. Lighting the hissing gas, he sat back down with the RT and resumed the task given him by corporal Macbeth.

The static turned to the melodic strains of a big band as he tuned the receiver knob, and he listened as a dance tune lifted his spirits. Violins drifted through the melody, but his revelry was suddenly interrupted as the signal started to fade and Simms found he had to adjust the large dial by minute amounts to keep the big band playing. Eventually, they faded away to be replaced by hissing static in the centre of his head. With practiced perseverance the young soldier adjusted the Bakelite knob with the hand of a safecracker, until he found the voice of an angel, singing a haunting song that, after a few minutes, seeped into his lonely soul and brought a lump to his throat.

The voice was the most evocative sound that he had ever heard, a sort of American blues number. But She too, like the big band before her, faded and left him sitting in the middle of a humid forest watching a kettle boil on a primus stove. He tried to find her again, but in vain. All he found was Morse signals bleating out like a machine gun, mostly code numbers in groups of five. The black earphones were making his ears sweat, so he took a break. Unpeeling his spectacles, he wiped his damp, bony head down with his damp vest as he became aware of the steam starting to issue from the kettle's spout. He glanced over his shoulder, a habit he had adopted whenever Boyce was in the vicinity, to see what he was up to.

Boyce was now sitting cross-legged next to the wrecked lorry, cleaning his precious Thompson machine gun. He had stripped the weapon down to its component parts and was meticulously cleaning each piece with a petrol soaked rag. Boyce had been very secretive about his gun and wouldn't say where or how he had acquired the weapon, being a rare original model with front pistol grip, Cutts compensator and fifty round drum. The type used by gangsters in prohibition films.

Simms, reassured for the time being that he was not likely to be assailed, lay down and picked himself a long, succulent blade of grass and chewed. He looked up at the blue sky as the cloying heat drew the tension from his exhausted body as he drifted into a half slumber, the little kettle hissing quietly to itself beside him.

Boyce pulled through the barrel of the Thompson, applying a little light oil to the spring and other machined parts as he carefully reassembled the mechanism with the dexterity of a watchmaker. Running a finger of oil down the wooden stock, he worked it in with small circular motions until the grain was full, finishing it with a hard burnish, until the wood glistened. Working the freshly oiled action, he then loaded a full drum of fifty rounds and applied the safety.

Salvaged from the damaged lorry, Boyce turned his attention to a Boys antitank rifle and although there was no ammunition for it, he thought he would clean it anyway. Stripping the rifle down and laying all the parts out neatly on an old groundsheet gave him a certain satisfaction. The feel of the machined parts made with such tight tolerances and the way they all fitted together was something Boyce could appreciate. He admired the BSA gunsmiths that made it.

The Boys rifle was a heavy weapon with a padded shoulder stock and wooden cheek plate, and fitted with a Monopod to the barrel. Boyce unscrewed the top and applied oil to all the major parts, paying particular attention to the breech and removing any deposits he found there. As his laboured a red squirrel approached him, Boyce stayed perfectly still to see what the insignificant creature would do. The squirrel darted forward and stopped and then darted back again, circling around until it reached Boyce's ammo pile of acorns, whereupon it grabbed the nearest one and ran off.

'Cheeky bugger,' muttered Boyce under his breath. Presently the small rodent returned for another, while Boyce sat and watched as the squirrel depleted his cache one by one.

Simms startled back to the world from his fitful sleep to find insects crawling over his sweating face. Sitting up, he poured some lukewarm water over his head from his water bottle and then took a long swig of the tainted fluid. Draining the dregs, he gargled and spat out the residue, and hooking his specs over his luminous ears, he carefully removed the kettle from the stove and poured the boiling water into a mess tin containing loose, black tea leaves. Stirring the browning liquid with his WD spoon, he prepared two chipped enamel mugs and then ferreted in his pack for his cigarette tin. Extracting an unbroken Woodbine, he carefully tapped the end on top of the tin lid to compact any loose tobacco, before putting it to his lips and lighting it.

Just at the moment of ignition, a screeching fireball shot past him, slammed into a tree, rolled on a few more yards, and stopped. The burning fireball seemed to flare suddenly and then died down.

Simms, perplexed, just sat and stared at the smouldering mess. Getting to his feet, he walked over to the charred remains to take a closer look and caught a whiff of petrol, emanating from what Simms could now plainly see, as the blackened corpse of a small mammal. He looked back at Boyce. He stared back with a big grin on round face. 'You mad Sod,' shouted Simms. 'He was nickin' me nuts.' Boyce shouted back with a grin on his pasty face.

'I don't give a damn. You don't treat dumb animals like that.' Simms pointed at the smoking remains. 'It was an accident.'

'Accident, my arse, you're a bloody, sadistic cockney cunt.' Shouted Simms.

'The hell I am.'

'Fuckshite.'

Boyce walked over to inspect his handiwork. 'Did you hear the fucker squeal?' he said and winked at him.

Simms would not let himself be drawn, and knew it was pointless arguing with the feebleminded and went back to finish making the tea.

Boyce slid out his hunting knife and walked over to the charred remains, put the tip of his blade through the squirrel's blackened head and lifted it aloft.

'Fancy a little meat with your broth tonight, Simmo?' Boyce smiled, and then waited for Simms to look up before giving him another wink.

'You disgust me, you're sick in the head mate. Cretin.'

'I know that already. My mum always said I was abnormal.' Boyce looked wistfully into the trees.

'Destined for great 'fings she said. I am a bleedin' genius, Simmo. In my heart of hearts, I have always known that.' replied Boyce, as he tossed the cremated squirrel into the undergrowth. With a sense of bravado, he then suddenly turned, throwing the hunting knife at Simms. The knife cart wheeled and impaled itself in the trunk of a tree, a few feet away from Simms's head.

'You shit.' Simms jumped up and pulled the knife from the tree and made to throw it at Boyce, who turned and fled laughing.

Simms picked up his Enfield and worked the bolt. He raised the rifle to his shoulder and aimed it at the fleeing figure. Boyce was now looking worried and started to weave across the track, shouting obscenities back at Simms with threats to cut off his todger and fry it for dinner. Boyce ducked in behind a large tree. After a few moments, he showed himself and gave Simms the archer's salute of two fingers, dropped his trousers, and waggled his bare arse at him for good measure.

The bullet that Simms fired thwacked into the tree trunk a few feet from Boyce's bare buttocks, sending small shards of bark and splinters in all directions. Boyce dived for cover among the ferns, sending another flock of startled birds into the humid air. Boyce pulled up his trousers and slopped off on all fours to the edge of the ferns to peer out at Simms. His adversary was still holding the rifle and looking in his direction. Even Boyce knew when he had crossed a line and crawled off to find a shaded spot to hide for a while.

Adding the last of the powdered milk to his tea, Simms sat back down in the shade and powered up his radio. He thought he might try using the metal chassis of the mortified lorry to boost the signal, as the range of the set was only a few miles. As the set warmed up, Simms could hear the distinct sound of the Morse signals emanating from the phones, which were still lying on the ground. Sets of five letters, in random order that he could not decipher. He wrote down the sequence of letters as he understood it. His Morse was rusty, and he missed a few letters as the speed of the operator overwhelmed him. But he could decipher enough to know that the message was coded.

What did alarm him most was the fact that the transmitter sending these signals must have been very close by. He noted the frequency and turned the dial slowly one way and then the other. The signal was so strong that Simms even looked around the clearing, half expecting to see the operator waving at him. Then the signals suddenly stopped.

He held one earpiece up to confirm and listened to the faint static as he slowly turned the tuning knob, closing his eyes to concentrate his mind to the slightest variance in sound. Distant stations faded in and out, hissing classical music struggled in over the airwaves, the world service faded in giving out coded messages.

'St Paul will meet with Santa this evening.' 'St Paul will meet with Santa this evening.' Each phrase spoken with a clipped BBC voice that reassured Simms and reminded him of home.

A French woman sang patriotic songs to an accompanying accordion, the ballad slow and mournful. Music while you work. A big band played upbeat strains to tired workers' He tried to find the angel again, but she had vanished.

Glancing back down the track, for any sign of the corporal and the other men returning, all he could see was the tireless heat haze shimmering in the afternoon sun. They should have been back by now, he thought, 'Just a reccy down the track a way,' was Macbeth's parting remark. It was the uncertainty that aggravated him the most stuck here with Boyce?

He had to think of something else to occupy himself and sat down to repair some loose wires inside the radio. Above the swaying canopy, a gentle breeze brought a new sound. Boyce, who was skulking behind the lorry, noticed it first, a faint distant drone. Standing up, he moved out away from the lorry to hear better. He was surveying the sky above, trying to make out the new sound above the rustling tree top leaves. It came again, very faint but slightly louder, the unmistakable drone of aero engines.

Boyce walked further out into the middle of the clearing, looking up to the sky. He tried to gauge the direction that the planes were coming from, as the trees seemed to conspire against him, sending echoes around the glade in all directions.

Picking up his Thompson, he turned in slow circles, scanning the blue crevices between the leaves.

Simms had also heard the approaching aircraft. He peered over his metal-rimmed specs to see Boyce looking back at him, menacingly holding his Thompson and gesticulating with his thumb towards the sky. The drone of the engines seemed to pulsate, dropping off in volume and then rising again with the breeze.

Simms joined Boyce in the centre of the clearing, each scanning the strip of blue sky above as the sound grew louder. The deep drone of the aircraft engines gained in intensity as the two young soldiers circled around each other, as if in some pagan ritual, staring up to the heavens, straining to be the first to spot them.

Simms lifted his hand to point and was about to shout when he realised it was just a crow. He instinctively glanced at Boyce, who had noticed his error, and winked his annoying wink at him again. The big, black bird flew directly over them, and cawing its disapproval, defecated over Boyce's shaven head. The semi white fluid flowed down along the line of his scar and dripped down his back. Boyce, with characteristic zeal, opened up with short bursts from the Thompson while shouting obscenities at the unphased, cackling bird.

After the fifth burst, the sound of engines screamed to engulf them as the low-flying planes swept across the clearing. The sky seemed to explode with hot, roaring motors as the huge black bombers flew over, so low that they seemed to roll over the treetops themselves. With white and black crosses emblazoned on their wings, wave upon wave came on, turning the peaceful glade into a maelstrom. Simms covered his red ears with his clammy hands as he looked up at the planes. Little black bombs nestled under their black bodies like precious little eggs. The bombers flew over them like a swarm of fruit bats on a summer eve.

Boyce opened up on them, screaming at the top of his voice, as he emptied the magazine at the formation. The air was filled with bullets and blasphemy. As the tail enders passed over, the sound dissipated, leaving the two soldiers with ringing ears and the acrid smell of burnt petrol and cordite permeating their nostrils.

'I 'fink I hit that fucker, did you see smoke' shouted Boyce, laughing to himself.

'Yes, you got that one alright Boyce, it came down in flames.'

'Sod off Simmo, that planes going home with holes in it.' Laughed Boyce,

'You missed.'

'I hit it, I tell you.' said Boyce, reloading the Thompson. 'Where's my knife Simmo?' 'I dunno, you probably threw at someone.' replied Simms as he went in search of his tea. 'I want it back.'

'Where do you think the corporal has got to?' asked Simms, looking back down the track. 'How should I bleedin know.' Boyce felt his shaven scalp. His fingers came away covered in white and black excrement. 'Dirty black bleeders.'

'I see they've been at the blackberries again,' said Simms. Boyce wiped the guano from his head with the filthy, wet vest he had stolen from Simms earlier. Seeking revenge, he looked around the glade and spotted a large, fat crow alight on a limb, its head moving from side to side. The perch it was occupying suddenly exploded in splinters and showering leaves as Boyce gave it one long burst. The crow, unscathed, fell ten feet before it spread its wings and glided away, cawing his disgust as it went.

'We're supposed to conserve ammo.' Simms shouted over the din. 'Not when we are in contact with the enemy,' Boyce stood to attention and gave Simms a salute. 'Crows are not the damn enemy.'

'It was a Fokker. Anyway I'm not putting up with it, shitting all over me 'ed, story of me bleedin life that is.' Boyce looked up at Simms with a stupid grin on his face. 'always someone or something tryin to shit all over me. Where's that bleedin' tea then, mate?' 'Teas up.' Simms handed Boyce a chipped enamelled cup containing a grey fluid. 'About time.' Boyce looked at the tea and took a sip, 'Well, at least it wet and warm. Where did that bloke Witherspoon come from anyway Simmo, seems a right 'erbert to me?'

'I suppose, like the rest of us, he just got separated from his unit.'

'Big old bastard, though. One of them country bumkins.'

Simms emptied the dregs of his water bottle over his head to wash away the stale sweat. He longed for a cold shower and a good night's sleep in a comfortable bed. Removing his stiff, black boots, he rubbed his sore feet and tipped-toed over to the lorry to refill his water bottle from a rusty jerry can. Boyce came up behind him.

'So, where the hell do you think the corporal's got to Simmo?' before Simms could answer, Boyce had coughed up some phlegm in the back of his throat, and leaning back, he suddenly thrust his head forward ejecting the mucus in a high arc, landing some distance away with a dull splat on one of the crosses. The thick, yellow liquid slid down the centre post. 'Shot,' said Boyce, looking very pleased with himself.

'You really are something else.' said Simms, dryly. He padded back across the glade and started putting the radio back together. The transmitter valve was useless and needed a replacement. Cleaning all the connections with a spare toothbrush and tightening all the screws and bolts inside the hot, metal casing, he turned on the set and waited for the remaining valves to warm up. The radio crackled into life and hissed at him. Leaving the earphones on the ground, he could hear the wave changes, whistles, static and various stations trying to break through. Haw-Haw came and went, and finding nothing of interest, Simms turned off the set to conserve the batteries. He was thinking of a way to boost the signal by using the lorry chassis when Boyce shouted over.

'Get a load of this Simmo.' He was lying on the ground with his trousers down and his skinny, boot-clad legs in the air. In his hand he held a box of Swan Vestas and struck a match, which he then held close to his anal passage as he passed wind.

The resultant blue and yellow flame shot six feet across the glade. His petrol soaked trousers and socks caught fire, along with most of his pubic and bum hair. The burning, smouldering Boyce rolled around in the dry grass and undergrowth, which then also caught fire, leaving a trail of burning foliage in his wake. He desperately tried to pat the flames out and remove his boots and trousers while rolling around. His Khaki trousers were well alight by now, the flames licking enthusiastically at his already scorched scrotum. Screaming, he hopped around the lorry, pleading for help.

Simms watched the spectacle unfold in stony silence. The smell of burning wool and singed hair drifted over to him on the warm, light breeze.

Chapter 2.

Corporal Macbeth stood five feet four inches tall in his army boots. He was a thickset, muscular man with bright carrot orange hair, which stuck straight out from his head, as if attracted by a magnet. He rested under the shade of a tree, as he watched two lanky, dishevelled soldiers strolling up a track way towards him.

'Nothing down there corp,' reported Evans, a muscular ex bouncer from Cardiff. He removed his tin helmet, and wiping his forehead, added, 'Just peters out half a mile down.'

'What do you reckon, then?' asked Macbeth. 'Well, keep going down this main track, see where it goes.' replied Evans gesturing towards the track winding off through the trees.

'I don't want to get too far from the radio,' said Macbeth, scratching his sweaty crotch.

'We should have brought the other two with us,' replied Evans.

'We'll have to head back soon, Simms might have picked up something by now.' said Macbeth getting to his feet.

'I think that would be for the best, corporal, don't you,' said Witherspoon, a gentle giant of a man standing well over six and a half feet tall. 'Our trench line can't be far from 'ear corporal.' Macbeth was aware that Witherspoon was not the full ticket since they found him wondering about the forest looking for his unit. 'Yes, that's why I said it.' replied Macbeth, sardonically.

'Should never split your force when you don't know the disposition of the enemy,' muttered Evans sarcastically.

'What was that?'

'Nothing,'

'Well enough faffing about here, we'll head back,' said Macbeth, refitting his helmet and brushing the mud and dry leaves off his trousers.

'To be quite truthful, I think nothing has used this road, if you can call it a road, for some considerable time,' said Witherspoon, surveying the ground intently, 'in fact I would go so far as to venture that this part of the forest has been neglected and tis a pity.' He kicked at the hard surface with his boot and bent down to pick up a discarded horseshoe, incrusted with age and rust. 'If you ask me, we could be a wandering around these 'ere woods for days and….'

'Alright, I'm not asking your opinion, Witherspoon, am I,' barked Macbeth. 'This is not a debating society, we'd better start back.' Macbeth bowed and extended his left arm, 'After you Gentlemen' and ushered the two soldiers forward.

Evans looked at Witherspoon and said, 'We, just walked a mile up and mile down this bleedin' track, in this bleedin' heat while you have rested in the shade. Can't we have a breather for a few minutes before we start back?' 'All right, all right, ladies, have a little rest and powder your nose. Would you like tea and scones?' Macbeth said as he flipped his wiping cloth over his left forearm.

'Don't put yourself to any trouble on our account,' replied Evans dryly.

'I could just do with tea and scones right now,' muttered Witherspoon, taking the top off his water bottle. 'What say you Evan's?'

'It'll wait.' Evans sat down under a tree and offered Witherspoon a cigarette in compensation. The tall men smoked and talked together in subdued tones that Macbeth couldn't quite make out, which was to Macbeth a constant irritation that he believed the lower ranks did on purpose just to irritate him. The corporal stretched and made ready to leave, and jauntily headed back up the track.

The two tired privates reluctantly shouldered their rifles and moved off, following Macbeth. Witherspoon had made a sunhat from his handkerchief by tying a knot in each corner, which he now wore against the glare of the sun. The heat and humidity got to all of them now, sapping their strength. Macbeth, being fair skinned, glowed a peculiar shade of pink that complimented his orange hair, framed within his green helmet.

Feeling the weight of his water bottle, Macbeth estimated that only a third remained, and they had not come across any water source since leaving the clearing. The few remaining jerry cans would not last long.

Water, he knew, was as important as ammunition for keeping up moral and it was up to him to provide it. He looked back down the track to see Evans and Witherspoon ambling along, like a couple of Bohemian poets out for a Sunday morning constitutional, and muttered under his breath about the state of the British soldiery.

Evans tramped along in his lace less, hobnailed boots, the crutch of his khaki trousers hung down between his knees allowing his bracers to bounce back and fore against his calves and his army vest had become so soiled that it was difficult to distinguish grimy material from grimy skin. Witherspoon was a shambling mess. Only he wore his handkerchief cap on his shaved head and puttees above his boots.

Macbeth stopped to take a swig of tepid water from his water bottle, allowing Evans and Witherspoon to close up and pass him. They ambled up the track a way, before coming to a standstill and leaning on their rifles. They chatted amiably while they waited for the little corporal to catch up.

As he approached the two giants, he offered them a swig each from his water bottle. They stood over him, waiting. Macbeth became uncomfortable, as he had always felt a little intimidated by tall people. He preferred to keep a space around himself that no one should impinge upon, especially lanky privates. Evans and Witherspoon, being unaware of this basic rule, now stood over the little corporal. 'Stand back you lot for fuck's sake let me have some space here will you.' The hot and bothered corporal handed over his water bottle to Evans. 'Thanks corp, I'm all out.' said Evans as he took a swallow of the tepid water. He passed the water bottle to Witherspoon.

'Its too bloody hot to mess about,' said Macbeth.

'Who's mucking about, then?' Evans replied, wiping his forehead with the bottom of his vest.

'Witherspoon, get that stupid, bloody hanky off your head. Where's your helmet, man?'

'I got it right here corp, hangin' off me belt like, I thought me 'anki would be cooler than me helmet is getting uncomfi like.'

'Alright, keep it on for now, but if an officer turns up, whip your helmet on the double,' said Macbeth, inching over to the other side of the track.

Evans looked up and down the deserted road.

'How the hell are officers going to turn up here?'

'You never know, just be aware and keep your wits about you.'

'Where do we go from here then?' Witherspoon put in, 'I rather think ussun's are lost, and we need to get back to our trench line. We could end up a wanderin into some Hun trench instead.'

'Don't get the wind up, chum, the corporal will get your lanky arse home,' said Evans, tucking in his damp vest and adjusting his rifle strap, which was chafing his collarbone.

Witherspoon looked over at Evans, and they both smiled. 'I ain't got no wind up to be sure Evans, I thought that the corporal might need some 'elp is all.'

'I am standing here you know, and don't come the old soldier with me Witherspoon,' said Macbeth, 'and when I need your 'elp, as you put it, I'll let you know.' Trickles of sweat ran down his pink face as he turned to address Evans.

'What do you reckon then, Evans?' enquired Macbeth, squinting back over his shoulder.

'Pick up the others and then head south corp. Keep going in one direction, we're bound to come out somewhere. We could just walk towards the sound of the Artillery.'

'They be behind our lines.' Said Witherspoon. Macbeth cupped a hand to his ear. 'What artillery? Can you hear any guns, Evans?

Anyway, they could be enemy guns.' Macbeth looked down at his dusty boots and thought about Evans's proposal, which he agreed in principle was a good idea, but he would not say so. 'I'll think about it, Evans. Well, it's time to get back before those two blighters kill each other.'

Evans just smiled at Witherspoon as he moved his rifle over to the other shoulder. Witherspoon rang the sweat out of his hanky cap and slid it back over his head. Macbeth led the way up the rutted road, his little legs working twice as fast to keep ahead of Evans and Witherspoon. The three soldiers marched on up the hot, winding road, ferns and endless trees on both sides. And it wasn't long before Macbeth's legs tired and faded. He stopped to take stock and muttered some curses to himself as the lanky privates passed him. He averted his eyes as he knew the pair would grin their stupid grins at him.

'Heat getting to you corp?' asked Evans as they passed.

'No.' barked Macbeth.

After another mile or so Macbeth, sweating profusely in the fetid air, caught up with Evans and Witherspoon. They were crouched down on the road, observing something ahead. 'What's up?'

Evans pointed up the road. 'Up there corp, just to the left of that fallen tree, see 'im?' 'No.'

'A bleedin' great dog, there by the tree, see 'im, looking right at us,' repeated Evans.

Macbeth strained his little piggy eyes. He couldn't see anything. 'Where?' 'Bleedin Nora, he's standin' right there, man. A hundred yards up the road. You need bloody specs corp.' As Evans pointed again, the animal walked casually across the gravel road.

'Now I see him, ' said Macbeth with relief. He dragged his rifle round. 'I'll pot the bugger.'

'Hang on a minute, he could be important, ' said Evans, holding the barrel of Macbeth's

Enfield. 'Do you reckon?'

'The dogs carrying something in panniers at his sides. Look again?' asked Evans. 'I like dogs I do.' said Witherspoon to no one in particular.

'We'll 'ave to get closer. Could be with a Woodsman or something,' replied the corporal with an air of authority.

The three soldiers sidled slowly up the road, fanning out as they went. Evans whistled and patted his thigh, calling the dog to him.

The confused German Shepard stood in the middle of the road and eyed them cautiously, his tongue lolling out of its open jaw.

They got within twenty yards of him before he became skittish and backed off a little. All three stopped and crouched down on the track

.Macbeth eyed the dog and said, 'It's a bloody German breed.' The dog stood in the middle of the track and eyed Macbeth back. He wore a canvas harness with leather panniers fixed to each side. Sticking up from the centre of the harness was a wooden rod about a four inches high. Witherspoon looked at Evans quizzically and said, 'I think that's just the breed corp, a German Shepard. I think General French has one of them back in Blighty.' 'Who the Hell is General French when he's at home? That mutt looks like one of them Alsatians,' whispered Evans.

'What do you think the bugger is carrying in those side panniers?' asked Macbeth. 'And what is that wooden rod sticking up for?'

'Dunno. Could be maps or important documents. The wooden rod thingy probably had a little flag on it or something to identify it.' replied Evans.

After a few minutes, the dog raised its head and sniffed the humid air before trotting off into the trees.

Macbeth slid his boiling helmet off his boiling head and soaked up the sweat with his spare long Johns, rubbing his head all over until his spiky hair sprang out, making his head look like a ginger mollusc.

'What be that harness thing on his back then, corporal?' enquired Witherspoon. 'I'd never seed that afore today. What say you Evans,

'Ave you seed anything like that in you life afore today?'

'No. I've never seed that afore today' Mimicked Evans.

Witherspoon looked at Evans in consternation. You takin' the piss mate?'

'No, well a little, sorry Witherspoon. No offence meant'

'No offence taken, if no offence was meant like,' said Witherspoon. 'I could understand the corporal yer sayin that, 'cos that's what he's like. But I didn't expect it from yo' Evans, as I thought we as mates.'

'Alright, when you ladies have finished, can we get back to the mutt' interjected Macbeth.

'Sorry corporal, but this yer 'eat is gettin me all salty like,' said Witherspoon. 'I be a missin me Funk hole'

Macbeth took a deep breath. ' There is only one way to find out. We will have to capture the mutt and relieve him of his cargo.'

Well, if he won't come to heal we are going to have to shoot him.' replied Evans.

'We can't shoot the poor dog, he don't know no different.' said Witherspoon.

'I want to see what that bloody dog's carrying.' said Macbeth as he walked down the road to the spot where the dog had entered the forest and peered in.

'If he says anything about pincer movements, I'll do for 'im,' said Evans to Witherspoon, as the two soldiers moved up to where Macbeth was creeping into the trees. The three soldiers squatted on their haunches, surveying the scene before them. 'What's the plan of attack then, corp?' whispered Evans.

Macbeth gestured to the others to form a huddle and then whispered his plan to capture the enemy dog. 'We will split up and form a half circle. Witherspoon, I want you in the middle, as the bleedin dog lover, to entice the bugger, have you got anything to entice him with?'

Witherspoon opened his pack and pulled out a tin of corned beef. 'This should be alright corporal.'

'Evans, you and me will take the flanks and form a pincer movement, ok.' Witherspoon laughed.

'What so bloody funny?' 'Scuzy corporal, It be nothing. Do you have a can opener andy to open this er tin?' said Witherspoon earnestly.

'I've got one in my pack. Do you want an enamel plate to put it on?' asked Evans. 'What the hell is this? Have you got a bloody lead in there as well Evans, we could all take it walkies afterwards.' scowled Macbeth as he pulled out two Mills bombs from his haversack and clipped them to his chest pockets.

'Are we going to capture it or blow it to pieces?' Evans enquired.

'I'm just taking precautions in case that mutt takes off. If he does, I want you to shoot the bugger.'

'I'd rather not hurt the dog if it's all the same to you corporal, I'm rather found of dogs 'avin had one as a pet. I raised 'im from a little puppy, you see. Oh, I must have been…'

'Let's get on with it,' interrupted Macbeth.

'Oh, yes, alright, only I was going to add his name was Stinky, owing to the fact that he did fart a lot, even as a pup, bless 'im.'

'Have you finished?'

'Yes corporal, mind you, me Ma wouldn't have the little cunt in the house.'

'Evans to the right, then. I'll go left.' whispered Macbeth and moved off through the trees and disappeared.

Witherspoon made his way in through the trees. Opening his tin of corned beef, he waved it in the air to help the aroma of the fluid beef drift on the small breeze. 'Here boy, look what I 'ave 'ere for ye.' The smell of the beef pervaded the area as Witherspoon crept forward in his metal studded boots, trying not to make too much noise. He added a little whistle between calls.

'Come on yo little rascal, come and get yer eats,' called Witherspoon, followed by a long, two-tone whistle. Macbeth and Evans, having taken up their positions, watched as Witherspoon wooed and waved the tin. Macbeth, parting the ferns in front of him, scanned the area for any sign of the dog. Presently, the dog emerged from the gloom into the clearing, sniffing the air and licking his chops. Witherspoon placed the serrated tin down and, still coaxing, backed off to allow the dog to get at the food.

Macbeth saw Evans closing in on the other side of the clearing and gesticulated to him to jump on the animal and wrestle it to the ground. Evans gesticulated back with two fingers. Macbeth cursed the undisciplined Welshman and made a mental note to put him on a charge at some point in the future. He decided that he would have to do the job himself, and with this in mind, he put his rifle aside and went down on all fours and crept through the ferns. The grenades swung from his chest like little lethal breasts as he made his way forward.

The dog glanced nervously over as Macbeth appeared from the ferns pretending to be a dog, mimicking the idiosyncrasies of the species. The Alsatian, now alarmed, pricked up its ears and, sensing the encirclement, ran off through the trees. In its panic to escape, the animal ran past Macbeth, who sprang at the frightened beast and fell over a fallen tree. He landed heavily on the ground. The impact took the wind out of his lungs and he lay prostrate, face down in the wet moss, unable to move. The corporal turned blue as he struggled to inflate his lungs, and panic was now manifesting in his brain as Evans ran over to assist him. Rolling the little man over, Evans failed to notice, as one of Macbeth's grenades snagged on a twig, releasing the pin and sending the safety lever springing off into the air. There followed one of those moments as the two soldiers looked at the fizzing bomblet, which had now dropped to the ground, and was about to explode.

Evans picked up the grenade and tossed it into the ferns. It went off with a dull thump, sending sods and leaves into the air. The corporal closed his eyes and gasped in some air at last.

Evans laughed, 'That was a close one, are you alright corp?'

Macbeth made a plaintive cry as his lungs reinflated, his face turning back from bluish purple to red as Evans helped him to sit up. Witherspoon gave him a drink from his water bottle, and removing his tunic from his pack, he made him a pillow to rest his head.

'I be glad we didn't have to hurt the dog. Poor thing looked frightened to death. I think that's the last we see of 'im.' said Witherspoon. 'Sod the flea-bitten mutt,' said Evans, collecting his rifle. He knelt down and looked at Macbeth. 'You alright to make a move corp?' Macbeth looked up at Evans and nodded.

'I think we have company,' said Witherspoon, looking over his shoulder.

Standing among the ferns stood a German soldier. He wore a grey greatcoat and a helmet that looked two sizes too big for him. He stood among the ferns with his arms in the air. Evans raised his rifle and pointed it at the stranger, gesturing to him to come forward into the clearing, which he did, and as he stepped out of the ferns, they could see that he was wearing Wellington boots under the greatcoat. 'Kamerad.' The German soldier shouted, looking nervously from one to the other.

Evans and Witherspoon instinctively spread out, rifles at the ready, apprehensive at the sudden appearance of the enemy in their midst.

'Kamerad.'

As Evans approached the surrendering soldier, he made him put down his arms and take off his helmet and open his greatcoat. The man did as he was bid and placed his helmet slowly down on the ground, careful not to make any sudden movements, and stood up again. His filthy, shaven head shone with sweat. 'Kamerad.'

'Alright Fritzie boy, we are nine Kameraden to you mate.' Evans said waving his hand from side to side. He gestured to the German to open his greatcoat. The bewildered soldier unbuttoned the coat and opened it up.

Evans looked at the naked, emaciated body, covered in sores and bruises. Dried diarrhoea stains ran down the inside of his legs. He exuded an overwhelming stench.

'Bloody Nazi's, they rot from the inside out,' said Evans. 'Why do you think he's wearing that big old coat, then?' asked Witherspoon. 'Dunno, maybe its to keep the stink in,' Evans made the prisoner button the coat back up. He gingerly patted the coat pockets to check that he had no hidden weapons.

'Kamerad' the German soldier gestured to Evans's water bottle. 'Wasser.' Evans handed him his water bottle, and the Nazi soldier drank the tepid water with relish. 'That's enough, Adolph.' said Evans, snatching back his water bottle. The emaciated soldier just looked at them with his piercing grey, frightened eyes. Macbeth had recovered sufficiently to stand up. He breathed in, filling his lungs, and exhaled. Walking over, he looked the prisoner up and down and offered him a cigarette, which the German accepted gladly. Macbeth felt slightly more at ease with the vile man as he was about the same height as himself. He lit the cigarette for him.

' Danke, Kamerad.'

'Shoot the fucker,'ordered Macbeth nonchalantly. 'You shoot him,' replied Evans.

'Witherspoon, you shoot him, and that's an order.'

'Well, if it's all the same to you, I would rather not. Just look at the poor bugger, he's in a worse state than we are.' replied Witherspoon.

'Well, what are we going to do with him?' replied Macbeth.

Witherspoon looked the German over from a distance, and said, 'This old boy stinks worse than my old dog, Stinky.' Where do you think he got them their Wellies from?'

'I don't give a rat's arse where he got the bloody Wellies from.' Macbeth started to get irritated. 'Let's just get rid of him and move on.'

'Well, you'll have to do the deed yourself corp.' Evans shouldered his Enfield and sauntered off.

'He's your prisoner Evans, He's your responsibility.'

Evans turned around and glared at Macbeth

'My responsibility, my arse. If it's down to me, just let the bugger go. It's not that he can do us any harm. Look at the state of him?'

The corporal backed away, knowing Evans was right. He recovered his rifle, and, just to have the last word said, 'don't blame me when his mates turn up to do us all in. Then we'll see who's in the shit.'

'Didn't know Fritz had Wellies, is all.' Witherspoon gave the German the opened tin of corned beef, which by now was crawling with flies. The German soldier emptied the contents down in one gulp and discarded the empty tin. They left the reeking Nazi standing in the clearing and made their way along to the gravel track. After a couple of hundred yards, Witherspoon looked back and saw the German soldier following them. 'He's

following usun's, he be.'

Macbeth looked back down the track,

'Christ, he's taken a shine to you Evans, your

Kamerad can't leave you alone.' said Macbeth, sarcastically.

'Nazi fucker, if he didn't look so pathetic I would shoot him.' Evans walked back down the road towards the German soldier, and as he approached him, the German put his hands up. 'Kamerad.'

'Fuck off, Fritz, you can't come with us.' Evans made the pathetic man put his arms down and sit on the ground.

'Tis a rum affair, that there Fritz 'avin no undergarments an all. Looked like he's bin in the wars, so to speak,' said Witherspoon, 'I feel a bit sorry for 'im, poor bugger.'

'Don't get sentimental about this Nazi fuck. Remember why were're here Witherspoon, he'd as soon slit your throat as look at you,' said Macbeth.

'I find that 'ard to believe corporal, he be nothing but skin and bone like.'

Macbeth looked on as Evans threw the German a pack of cigarettes. Flies had gathered around the seated prisoner in such profusion that he appeared to have a moving, black aura about him. 'I'm glad we didn't shoot the poor bastard. We can't get ourselves as low as they. '

Witherspoon mused, 'anyway can't see as he will last much longer.'

Evans returned, leaving the German sitting in the middle of the road.

'I think he's got the idea now corp.' said Evans.

Macbeth looked down the road at the pitiable heap. The little corporal came up to his full height and said, 'right then lads let's show this Nazi bastard how the British Army marches.' Macbeth came to attention and shouldering his Enfield, marched off down the track, bringing up his right arm to level on each movement as if on parade back in Aldershot. He shouted left, right, left right as he went, assuming Evans and Witherspoon were right behind him.

The Nazi sat on the ground, a packet of Players in one hand, and a water bottle in the other, and watched them go. He waved his hand to brush the flies away, which had gathered in clouds to irritate him.

As Macbeth marched away up the track, shouting orders to himself, Evans and Witherspoon ambled along after him. The squatting German soldier watched them go and eventually disappear as they rounded a bend. He looked up at the blue sky as black bombers streamed overhead.

Chapter 3

Private Boyce gently applied a liberal amount of warm, rifle lubricating oil to his reproductive parts. The oil felt soothing as it slipped into his red, sore crevices and washed away the oozing puss that had accumulated around his groin.

He gently massaged his raw foreskin with his oily fingers and painfully pulled away some frazzled pubic hair still sticking to his basted scrotum sack.

After emptying the contents of his water bottle over his vest, he applied the sodden cloth to his midsection, giving instant relief as the heat dissipated. He tried getting to his feet, spreading his legs apart, like a new born foal, and inching backwards until he braced his back against a tree. He pushed with one foot and then the other until he stood, more or less upright.

Simms sat in the shade of a lime tree, being entertained by Private Boyce's antics. He had always found people watching fascinating. If, of course, Boyce could be included in that category. A strange thought strayed into his head that alarmed him enough to stop him masticating on his grass root and spit it out. A thought that he may have some macabre, voyeuristic tendencies towards the deranged. During one tedious history lesson he had read about the well to do visiting Lunatic Asylums for entertainment.

He pondered the question for a moment as he picked a fresh, white succulent grass root and popped into his mouth and concluded that, for the moment, he just took pleasure in seeing Boyce in pain.

Boyce, meanwhile, had moved slightly away from the tree and stood precariously wobbling back and fore. He tied the wet vest around his waist using the armholes and brought the sagging wet material up through his legs to form a loincloth. Once secured, he attempted forward locomotion and, like a baby taking its first steps, he swung his left leg out and then his right, grimacing at each effort and checking his balance after each movement. By this method, he covered several yards before stopping to rest. His face had turned the same shade of vermilion as his groin.

Sweating profusely and hunched over, he looked like an old man suffering from ulcerated haemorrhoids. With curses and groans, he changed tack and moved sideways towards Simms, developing the gait of a gorilla.

'Help me out Simmo, me ol' mate. I'm in agony 'ere,' pleaded Boyce.

'You look somewhat knackered, Boycey.' 'Have you got any morphine for me, mate?'

'I've got something better than that for you, Boyce me ol' mucker.' Simms held up a .303 round.

'Cunt'

Boyce bent over and braced himself with one hand on each knee. He looked as if he was about to pass wind again, prompting Simms to move his location.

'Don't let another one go, you sod,' said Simms.

'I'm in agony 'ere, me bollocks are giving me Jip,' gasped Boyce.

'Court-Martial offence.'

'What?'

'Self-inflicted wound,' replied Simms as he walked across the clearing. He looked back at Boyce, who was doubled over and wheezing, and almost felt sorry for him.

The sodden, filthy vest hung off Boyce's bony hips like a week old nappy, and steam now rose from it in the sunshine. He tried to straighten up, accompanied by grunts and moans. He practiced waddling forward in the vain hope of gaining forward movement without disturbing his pulsating scrotum.

Simms moved away across the other side of the glade and sat under a tree to rest, the shade giving a little comfort against the unremitting sun. He picked a fresh grass root and sucked at the white flesh. His glasses had become tainted and smudged, so he peeled off the wires wrapped around his ears and attempted to clean them with spittle and a dock leaf. Occasionally looking up to view the blurred, oscillating form of Boyce cursing the world for his own stupidity. The Dock leaf seemed to make matters worse, so he pulled out a spare vest from his kit, and after applying a small amount of water, rubbed at the lens until all the smearing had disappeared. Holding the glass up to the light, he confirmed the cleanliness of the lens before wrapping the wire hooks back over his sore ears.

As his vision clarified, he saw Boyce making his wobbling way towards him. Simms cringed as Boyce came up and clung to a tree trunk to steady himself. Unfastening his loincloth, he let it drop around his ankles, exposing his rainbow coloured groin, which he then thrust to within a few inches of Simms's face. Boyce pointed with his grubby index finger at the bald, incandescent ball bag with a little fold of skin resting on top, masquerading as his penis.

'Get your mincers on this Simmo?' said Boyce in a piteously pathetic voice.

Simms looked up at the purulent mess displayed before him. The sight of Boyce's roasted goolies made him nauseated, especially as they were in such close proximity. He could still feel the heat exuding from the pungent, festering wound and thought the pain must be excruciating. Simms looked up into Boyce's bloodshot eyes. 'That looks sore?'

'I'm in agony, mate!'

'Witherspoon has all the medicines.'

'Can't you do something for me, please? I'm beggin you?'

'I'll have a look in the lorry, see if I can find something,' he lied. 'You had better lie down and keep that area bathed.' Simms got up and promptly moved off towards the lorry. 'Be back in a jiffy. You take it easy now.'

Climbing in the baking hot cab, Simms pretended to look for the first aid box, feeling Boyce's stare boring through the back of his head. How Boyce could not see the medical boxes strewn across the clearing he did not know, each with a green cross on the side.

The heat was stifling and unbearable in the cab, even with no glass in the windows, so when Boyce had slithered down the tree trunk, Simms clambered out the far side and hid under the chassis.

Boyce was beside himself with pain and found keeping the area cool seemed to help. He dripped more tepid water over his groin and, feeling the cooling liquid trickle down between his buttocks to the grass below, gave a sigh of relief. Glancing over towards the lorry, he couldn't see Simms and supposed he had been abandoned, yet again, to his fate.

He wished he could at least sleep for a while to escape the pulsating, agonizing pain he was in. As he lay in the shade feeling the gentle caress of the grass between his legs, he felt a slight tremble in the ground, followed by a rumbling noise in the distance, like an approaching train.

Simms had also become aware of the rumbling sound, and had come out from under the lorry and climbed onto the cab roof, looking off to the south. There, appearing above the tree line, he could just make out a pall of smoke.

'What the hell is going on, Simmo?' shouted Boyce

'There's black smoke some miles away.'

'Did you find anything in the lorry?'

'Must be where those sodding planes dumped their loads.'

'Can't stand this, Simmo.'

'Some poor bleeders must have copped the lot,' said Simms as he surveyed the distant plumb, now growing larger, like some airborne fungus. Flashes of red and yellow reflected off the low cloud, followed by a rumbling report seconds later.

'Did you find anything?' repeated Boyce. 'No'

'Christ all bloody mighty, I can't stand this much longer,' whimpered Boyce.

'Get some bloody backbone, man,' said Simms, enjoying himself, 'morale fibre.' 'I don't give a shit.' Boyce adjusted his posture. 'I just need a shot of morphine, or summat.'

'You'll have to wait for Witherspoon,' Simms added, 'me 'ol mate, me 'ol mucker. Anyway, I expect they'll be back soon.' 'Hope so,' whimpered Boyce, as he tried to make himself more comfortable against a log. He extricated a packet of cigarettes from his ammo pouch and, carefully snapping the oval cheroot in two, lit it. Blowing the cool blue smoke through his nostrils, he leaned back, drained and tired. He didn't even have the energy or inclination to swat the small black beetle crawling up his forearm, fighting its way through the maze of fine white hairs, its shiny little shell giving off hints of colour as it moved. Boyce, exhausted, dozed off, the stub still smouldering between his lips.

Somewhere in the distance Simms could make out the drone of aircraft. Two engine bombers by the sound of their collective hum. He did not know where the planes were as the sound reverberated around the glade. He studied the blue vista available to him within the confines of the glade and could see nothing save for a single asthmatic bird limping across the sky. The pulsating sound drifted away to be replaced by the chatter of birdsong and the caws of the ever present crows.

The smell of petrol was still heavy in the air as he slipped the top off his water bottle and drank the stale, tepid water as if it was the best, chilled champagne. His throat was so parched that it tasty like burnt toast. A sudden tiredness came over him and as he lay down under the lorry, the liquid stillness of the day enveloped him as he drifted away.

Macbeth led his band of brother's back towards the glade. He was not in a good skin. Evans and Witherspoon had taken to hanging back from him, putting just enough distance between him so that he couldn't hear their conversation, which was exacerbated by bouts of laughter. He knew they were talking about him.

Rounding a bend, the damaged lorry hove into view, much to Macbeth's relief, he quickened his pace. As he approached,

Macbeth came up behind the dozing Boyce sitting on the grass, his back leaning against a log, his head lolling forward. Laying down his Enfield, Macbeth crept up behind the slumbering soldier and, using his Commando training, he gripped one hand against the back of Boyce's neck, and then clamped the other over his mouth.

In unison, both men shrieked with pain. Macbeth, with the glowing embers of Boyce's cigarette caught between his fingers, did a little fire dance around the glade. He ranted, and he raved. Licking his wound, his tongue flicked between his fingers like a venomous snake.

Boyce was suddenly awoken from a fitful sleep, found, to his dismay, that he could not breathe. His lips on fire. He had also, at that moment, purely by reflex action, brought his legs together, catching his lolling scrotum in a vice. Tears welled up in his swollen eyes as he experienced multiple agonies all at the same time. His lungs got confused and didn't know whether to inflate or deflate as the shooting, excruciating anguish wracked his body. His lower face had gone numb and his lips were pulsating as he retched green bile into his mouth, which he now gagged on. Green mucus seeped from his nose and mixed with the salty tears running down his face.

Macbeth screamed at the same time as the smouldering cigarette burnt the delicate soft tissue between his fingers. He doused his hand with water from his water bottle, massaging the blackened web and filled the air with obscenities, mostly aimed at Boyce's mother.

Who it seemed had had intercourse with

Satan.

Witherspoon came to Boyce's aid and found him face down, his body rigid, lying on the dank, urinated grass. He rolled him over like a log to find Boyce's face turned blue and his eyeballs had disappeared. Witherspoon poured water over his face and Boyce reacted by gasping in air. His rib cage expanded, doubling in size, followed by a coughing fit that sprayed the bile and phlegm over the front of Witherspoon's battledress. Pouring more clean water over his patient's face,

Witherspoon washed the filth away. He opened his pack and took out some clean bandages, small jars, and bottles.

'Never mind about him, what about my hand, burnt to smithereens it is,' shouted Macbeth, holding up his right injured hand for everyone to see.

Evans came over to see what all the fuss was about and observed the now exposed, multi coloured groin on Boyce. 'What the hell happened to him?'

'He set fire to himself.' Simms replied, as he sauntered over from the lorry.

Witherspoon applied some cream to Macbeth's hand and Boyce's lips. He prised Boyce's legs apart to examine his groin area, and whistled. 'That looks nasty.'

'That's disgusting, cover it up quick.' said Evans, looking down into Boyce's purple crotch. 'The boys a lunatic,' ventured Macbeth. 'Should make a good soldier then,' said Simms

'Hold on young feller me lad, I'll sort you out a treat,' reassured Witherspoon as he applied a clean, damp bandage to Boyce's forehead to get his temperature down.

'Stupid bastard, nodding off with a fag in his gob,' said Macbeth as he nursed his burnt hand. He licked his would, the saliva soothing the burn, and then spat, 'Christ all bloody mighty, what the hell is in that cream?' Macbeth spat again, trying to rid his mouth of the obnoxious taste.

'That's for external use only corporal, you shouldn't go around takin' medicine willy nilly an all,' said Witherspoon, disapprovingly.

Boyce lay prostate on the ground and looked up at Witherspoon as he administered an syrette of morphine, grateful to the big man for his attention. The pain abated immediately, and he suddenly felt at ease with the world.

Witherspoon wetted a cotton winceyette flannel and cleaned his patient down with a tenderness and care you would not expect from a man of his size. Gently, he applied some soothing lotion to Boyce's upper thighs and, lifting his purple penis clear of his scrotum sack, carefully massaged the lotion into the sore skin. Boyce looked up at the ultramarine sky and found, to his astonishment, that he had no objection at all to another man holding his cock. Even more surprising, and somewhat alarming to Boyce as the morphine took effect, was the fact that it now began to harden. Witherspoon just smiled as he worked the soothing lotion into Boyce's expanding reproductive organ.

Dull thuds could be heard someway off in the distance and they could see some thin black smoke snaking up into the blue. Corporal Macbeth clambered up onto the lorry cab with the dexterity of a mountain goat, steadying himself on the sloping roof and gazed at the thin, black pall in the distance. 'Someone copped it alright. Must have been those Jerry planes we saw earlier.' he said, wrapping a bandage around his fingers. Evans clambered up to join him and gain a better view. 'What do you reckon, then?' Macbeth asked. 'Looks to me someone copped it right enough. We should help if we can, corporal.' replied Evans.

'Ok, let's get our kit sorted and move out,' ordered Macbeth from the lofty position on the lorry roof.

Evans, shielding his eyes with his hand, squinted at the column of smoke, drifting and dispersing with the gentle breeze. He already felt the anxiety filling his thighs and gut with what they were about to find. He had already seen the effects of bombing on soft flesh and dreaded seeing it all over again.

'What about bollock brain?' asked Evans, nodding at Boyce.

'He'll have to hike it like the rest,' said Macbeth, as he cautiously dismounted the lorry cab, nursing his pulsating hand.

Simms packed away his radio and stowed his personal gear, glad to be on the move again. Witherspoon lifted the soporific Boyce on his back, in a kind of fireman's lift, before falling in with the others at the centre of the glade. Evans volunteered to carry Boyce's kit and Thompson.

Macbeth lifted the heavy Boys rifle Boyce had been cleaning, and examined the intricate carving to the cheek plate, and wondered who the letters S.R.V. referred to. The anti-tank weapon was too heavy to carry, so he just left it where it was. They filled their water bottles from the jerry cans off the lorry before they left.

With the troop mustered, the little corporal led the unit out of the clearing towards the billowing black stain some miles distant.

He felt a new confidence now, as he had somewhere to go, somewhere to lead his men. The rag-tag troop rattled along in single file, enamel cups and other paraphernalia clonked and banged together, echoing through the trees.

Macbeth, bringing up the rear, saw his little band now as a guerrilla unit, fighting for survival behind enemy lines, a hit and run combat squad. All this clonking and banging could be heard half a mile away. He made a mental note to sort it out at the next brew halt. He quickened his pace, his little legs working hard to get past Witherspoon, whose lumbering labouring gait and the wildly swinging legs of Boyce forced him out from the single path and into the low ferns hampering his progress. He saw his opportunity to pass as the path widened out slightly ahead, and he made a dash for it, passing the laden Witherspoon before the ferns closed back in again, forcing him behind Simms.

Boyce, doped up to the eyeballs, his head swaying and bobbing from side to side on Witherspoon's back, mumbled something about apples and pears and story. The little corporal was now sweating profusely as he slipped in front of Simms and led the way, at last, towards the black nimbus.

The path they were following meandered through the trees, sometimes taking them away from their intended route, much to the chagrin of Macbeth, who could do little about it. His head throbbed with vexation as the trek became gruelling in the cloying heat, so he called a halt and allowed the weary band to rest.

Boyce was placed carefully down under a tree away from the glaring sun and now becalmed, laughed and chuckled to himself before slipping into unconsciousness.

Evans and Witherspoon lit up and sat on their packs in the shade of an Elm and chatted amiably.

Wiping his face with his vest, Simms swallowed the dreary dregs of his water bottle and scratched at various parts of his body.

The lice were feeling frisky and seemed to multiply apace. He extracted his cigarette tin and, after tossing one over to Macbeth, he quenched his thirst and lit up, drawing the sweet blue down to bite at his throat and larynx. The nicotine soothed his addiction. Uncovering the canvas front, he plugged in the headphones and switched the set on, adjusting the tuning knob to the known frequency as he waited for the valves to warm up.

The Morse dots and dashes came in stronger than ever and he had to hold the earphones away from his ears because of the volume. Glancing up, he saw Macbeth looking at him pensively. He gestured for the corporal to join him.

Macbeth listened to the signals himself as Simms explained their significance. He nodded and paced up and down a few times and then sat down to fidget. He turned to

Simms and asked, 'Could it be coming from

our lot?'

'No, this stuff is encrypted. I can't make head nor tale of it,' replied Simms, wiping himself down. 'All I know is that this signal is very strong and the operator must be transmitting within a mile or so.' 'What signals?' asked Evans.

'Fritz is sending coded stuff, but the bugger is close.' Simms put the phones away and secured the canvas front.

The little corporal, with a look of concern on his face, stared up the road ahead. 'If Jerrie is that close, we had better keep a good eye out. You lot, stow anything that will make a noise.'

'The signal could be coming from anywhere nearby, so keep your peckers peeled.' said Macbeth, then added, 'Keep your damn safety catches on, I don't want any careless discharges from you lot.' 'Okey,

cokey corp.' said Simms.

As the men were gathering their gear together Evans pointed down the track.

'Blimey, cop a load of that, look you,'

Crossing the furrowed road ahead the men gazed at four ostriches as they made their way across. The soldiers stood in wonderment at such a sight. The flightless birds disappeared into the trees leaving the track empty again. 'Where the hell did they come from?' Evans asked.

'They probably farm them around here for the eggs, they make bleedin big omelettes I'm told,' said Simms, sarcastically.

They moved off, rattling packs were reslung, and the stupefied Boyce was hoisted aloft and strapped over Witherspoon's shoulder.

They fell in on the narrow track behind the diminutive corporal and marched out in single file. He ordered the troop to stay ten feet apart. Macbeth, despite his short, stubby legs, set a fast pace and presently they dropped into a shallow valley, which made their progress easier. There were muttered speculations in the ranks as to what they would find at the bombsite. Macbeth told them all to shut up.

At the bottom of the valley, they came to a languid amber stream, blissfully cold, fed from distant mountains. The mournful current only churned up to torrents when it hit immovables or squeezed its way through narrow gaps between rounded, yellow boulders. Macbeth waded in, and even though the water barely reached his knees, he held his rifle over his head.

Evans and Witherspoon, once water was sighted, dumped Boyce unceremoniously on the bank and, ignoring the biting midges, jumped in. The initial dunking in the cold water took their breath as they rolled away on the gravel bottom.

Simms followed on, once he had secured his radio and removed his helmet, boots and glasses. Before venturing in, he dipped his toe in the water and shuddered, but he was so hot and drenched with sweat that the only way in was to hold his nose and jump.

After the numbing the relief was exhilarating. He held his head under the water, and keeping his eyes firmly shut, he blew air through his nose until his lungs gave out, forcing him back to the surface. Lying on his back, he allowed the under current to take him downstream to the boulders, where he wedged himself between two rocks, allowing the rushing water to pass through him, cleansing his entire body. Simms laid back and looked up at the blurred sky.

Evans, who had jumped in fully clothed, helmet and all, sat on the bottom. He let the undertow lift him and, weightless, drifted along with the current, startling a few gudgeon along the way, until he foundered upon the rocks. He lifted both feet out of the maelstrom, exposing the lace less hobnailed boots to the afternoon sun.

Witherspoon just sat in a sheltered eddy, water up to his neck, smiling quietly to himself and enjoying the unexpected bath.

Boyce had regained semi-consciousness to find himself being eaten alive by midges. He stared at the tiny insects crawling all over his stomach. They poured out of his belly button and he didn't feel a thing. It was as though he was looking at someone else's torso. He then noticed the water. He thought he was hallucinating until he saw Evans float by.

Like an agile crocodile, he slithered over the bank and slipped under the water. After a few minutes, when he hadn't surfaced, Witherspoon pulled him out, pumped him out and gave him the kiss of life. He laid him gently back on the grassy bank, naked, his loincloth lost in the river. As he dried out the midges circled.

After some cajoling and threats, Macbeth assembled his bathers and, after filling their water bottles with fresh water, they fell in on the gravel track.

Witherspoon tended to Boyce, fanning away the squadrons of midges before applying more ointment to his groin and fashioning a relatively clean loincloth from an old vest.

The morphine had started to lose its potency. Boyce was helped to his feet and although a little unsteady at first, he waddled forwards reasonably well. With his recent immersion and clean loincloth, he was looking almost dapper. Witherspoon helped him on with his boots and after double knotting his laces, he staggered around the riverbank looking more like a drunken Greek god.

'Look at the state of that,' Macbeth muttered to himself, 'the finest army in the world.'

Boyce tagged on the end as the rest of the men moved off. Simms was volunteered into carrying Boyce's kit, as well as the radio. The refreshed troop moved out with extra gusto.

Macbeth held back to take up the rear and have a last look round, and as he slung his rifle, he noticed a movement further downstream, beyond the boulders. As he peered down river, two hyenas came padding out of the trees and waded into the water. One of them stopped halfway across and seemed to stare back at him. Macbeth looked on incredulously and then turned to call Evans back to verify what he was witnessing, but the other soldiers were too far away.

The two hyenas drank and climbed out, shaking the water from their fur, the sun glinting off the water droplets. The animals melted away through the trees as the little corporal marched off to re-join his men.

Simms wished he hadn't been coerced into carrying Boyce's equipment, as he already had the radio to haul and his own kit. Wringing wet and flagging, he stopped, and raising one hand protested, 'Hold up there, I can't keep this up all day,'

Without looking around, Witherspoon replied, 'you can have a rest soon Simmo.'

'How soon?'

'Soon'

'How soon is soon?' 'Soon.'

'Stop the banter, you lot. I'll let you know when we stop,' called Macbeth from the rear.

'This stuff is gettin bloody heavy, corp. My arms are falling off.'

'Stop your winging Simms, Boyce would do the same for you.' Simms looked back at the shaven headed, skinny boy in his nappy, wobbling up the track. 'I bet he wouldn't,' Simms muttered under his breath.

Evans, who had taken point, now held his arm up to stop the troop. The soldiers stood stock still. Macbeth came up to see what was going on. Evans whispered that something was coming up the track, just out of sight round a bend. Macbeth strained his ears to listen. He could just make out some distant creaking and rattling sound. The corporal gave the order to disperse, and they silently moved off the track and hid among the ferns.

Macbeth crawled forward through the foliage, elbowing his way past Witherspoon to seek a better vantage point. They discarded haversacks as bolts were worked and fresh rounds loaded. The soldiers squatted among the ferns bracing themselves as flies hovered in the windless air, looking for a way in to the sweating heads and being foiled by metronome hands.

As the men peered over and through the evergreen. Fern throngs touched their faces with spectral fingers, sticking to the salt laden sweat, and there was a reek of rotting vegetation in the air. Each man could smell the stale odour from their foul uniforms and feel the lice as they moved around the hairy parts of their bodies.

Constant sweat salt had made eyelids sore, and it was easier to keep them shut than open. Macbeth had started to shake a little, and it forced him to grit his teeth to hide it from the others. He noticed Simms licking his lips, trying to moisten his dry mouth. Glancing over his shoulder, he saw Boyce, completely naked apart from his boots, out on the track, urinating against a tree.

'What the hell is that cunt doing?' hissed Macbeth. 'I think the lad is still out of it corp, bless him,' ventured Witherspoon.

'I'll bless the fucker with my hobnail boot,' whispered Macbeth. 'Get that bleedin' dodger in here at the double.'

'Give us a hand, Evans, ' said Simms. The two soldiers snaked out of the ferns and grabbed an arm each, pulling Boyce back into the foliage.

Macbeth heard it first, a faint rhythmic noise floating through the trees.

'Can you hear that, Evans?'

'No'

'I can hear it now,' said Simms. 'What the hell is that?'

The sound became louder and was now accompanied by a soft, tinkling noise. 'Steady yourselves,' whispered Macbeth encouragingly.

The tension got palpable as each soldier waited, head down as the rhythmic, invidious noise came closer and closer.

Simms couldn't stand it any longer and was the first to break cover and stick his head up above the ferns, peering right up the path through his round, misted lenses.

'Well bugger me, it's just an old peasant woman,' he said.

Four more heads appeared above the ferns.

The black shape of an old perambulator came swaying down the uneven track, propelled by a little old woman. She was dressed from head to toe in black. A black headscarf wrapped over and around her head framed her wrinkled, leathery face. Her back was bent like a fishing pole under strain and she ignored the staring strangers as she passed.

Gripping the pram handle with her gnarled, bony hands, she steered the pram around potholes and roots with a concentrated dexterity as she muttered to herself. One buckled wheel squeaked with regularity on each rotation. Tin cans, chipped enamel cooking pots and cutlery hung over the side. The pram, filled with soiled bed linen and blankets, rocked and swayed with the tracks' undulations. Perched precariously on top, stood a small terrier dog, its bright eyes whisked from face to face, its ears folded back on its head. The little dog displayed a wonderful sense of balance as it rode the swaying bundle of clothing, its hindquarters oscillating against its wagging tail.

The soldiers just stood there among the ferns, looking on as she went on her way, oblivious, it seemed, to everything, and waited until she disappeared from view in the black caves formed by the relentless trees.

'I don't feel too chipper, corp,' said Boyce, scratching at his scabs.

'You go and lie down me ol' son, and I'll bring you a nice cup of tea.' replied Macbeth. 'Thanks corp.'

Slowly the troop gathered on the road and made ready. The bewildered Boyce staggered around among the ferns, trying to find his loincloth and kit. The soiled loincloth, which was smeared with ointment and dead midges, was recovered, doused with fresh water and donned.

'Call yourself a soldier, man,' said Macbeth with disdain.

'Who me corp?' replied Boyce.

'You are a disgrace to the British Army Boyce.' said Macbeth.

'Don't feel too good is all corp. I need to see the MO.'

'Witherspoon, I am placing private Boyce in your custody. Just keep the bugger in line, will you,' said Macbeth, stepping out on to the track.

Witherspoon agreed and gave Boyce a belt of medicine on the form of Brandy.

The thick black smoke had died down to a few wispy dark trails in the sky as Macbeth, eager to get going, hurried the men along. He turned to Boyce and looked up and down again. 'Are you fit to march with your equipment private?' asked Macbeth.

'Dunno,' replied Boyce.

'You either are or your're not.'

'Let me 'ave a go then corp,' he strapped his haversack on and with a few grunts and curses he fell flat on his back. He was picked up and set on his shaky way down the path again. His rocking gait took on the manifestation of early man.

'Fucking disgrace,' mumbled Macbeth, looking on, shaking his head.

'Can I have a bit more medicine, corp?' asked Boyce. The Brandy now infusing his

brain. 'Just sort him out, Witherspoon.'

Witherspoon gave the wounded soldier another quick swallow of Brandy. 'Strictly speaking, it's not medicine, but I thought it might dull the senses a little as usun's have such a lot of mar'chin to do,' said Witherspoon.

'What senses?' said Simms.

'Just give him more if it helps him move himself,' said Macbeth, getting irritated.

'Right you are, corp,' said Witherspoon.

'Simms, nip up that tree there and take a gander.'

'Why me?'

'Why not you,' retorted Macbeth?

'I don't like heights.'

'It's only a little tree.'

'No, it's not.' 'Just go half way up then,' pleaded Macbeth, sardonically.

'Why is it always me?' Simms muttered as he unloaded the RT and his kitbag.

'Your the agile one, you were made to climb trees.' said Macbeth looking up into the canopy of a large Oak.

'Stop monkeying about Simms, and get up the tree,' said Evans, lighting a cigarette. 'Very funny'

'I want the best man for the job Simms, and that is you.' ordered Macbeth.

Simms capitulated, relieved to take the weight off his back. Evans offered a leg up to gain purchase of the lower branches. He made his way up the trunk with trepidation, alighting on a thick branch fifteen feet off the ground. He tried not to look down, but did, turning his legs to jelly. Clinging to the main trunk, he made himself as comfortable as possible before surveying the panorama before him. Stretched out, as far as he could see, was the vast forest, all shades of green, mixed with blues and purples shimmering in the afternoon haze. Shrouds of mist enveloped the canopy in places, toying and caressing the white clouds above.

'Well, what can you see?' Macbeth shouted from below.

'Wait a minute,' replied Simms, trying very hard not to look down at him.

Partially obscured by leaves, he saw that there were several small columns of smoke drifting up through the trees a mile or so distant.

'Can't see much at all.'

'You must be able to see some bloody thing,' said Macbeth. 'I'm coming down.'

'Stay up there, Simms, and tell me what's going on?'

Simms descended slowly. He stuck to the main tree like a limpet, inching his way down, grazing his arms and legs against the bark.

Evans helped him down the last section. 'I'm not doing that again,' exclaimed Simms, spitting and spreading saliva on his cuts. 'Well, what did you see?' Macbeth was now getting vexed.

'Well nothing, just some smoke drifting from the trees, a mile or so over there.' he pointed in the general direction.

'Bloody lot of good you are,' said Macbeth, walking away. 'You go up then, if you think you could do better.' Macbeth turned round.

'I don't need to. I'm in command.'

'Command my arse.' muttered Simms.

'What was that, Simms?'

'Nothing.'

Macbeth reddened slightly before barking the order to move out. Witherspoon had creamed and dressed Boyce's balls and retied his loincloth.

The troop moved out and made their way towards the distant smoke. Witherspoon helped Boyce along as best he could. However, they fell behind and Macbeth was reluctant to wait for them and pressed on. It wasn't long before they smelt the fetid smoke drifting on the lazy air, permeating their nostrils and dry throats. Macbeth gestured to his men to keep vigilant and check their weapons as they neared their destination.

The sound of the forest had changed imperceptibly as they converged on the bombsite. The track formed a T junction with a partially tarmacked road. A silence had fallen, giving way to unnatural noises of crackles and the terrible sounds of hot metal renting and buckling. Macbeth could see a dark shape hanging from a Yew and found it to be the remains of a donkey, its head and one of its front legs missing. They moved away from the track and into the trees to avoid a pool of blood and the corpse of a dead horse.

Acrid smoke drifted around them, making their eyes sting even more and forming a fog so dense that their vision was curtailed to only a few yards. The troop covered their mouths and noses as best they could because of the stench.

 Several damaged vehicles were scattered along the road, some overturned and burning, while others had been destroyed. The larger parts, engines, back axles, and wheels were strewn around. A saloon car was lying on its side, half in and half out of a ditch. Its rubber tyres were burning fiercely, giving off a thick acrid smoke. They moved away to gain fresh air. Intermittent puffs of flame appeared within the dense, black smoke like giant fireflies, and the heat from the corrupted vehicles kept the soldiers at a distance.

 The full stench of the place now overwhelmed them. A mixture of burning rubber, diesel and cooked flesh filled the humid, fetid air. It seemed that all the flies in the forest had come to feast and lay their eggs as they buzzed and skitted around their heads. A dead dog lay near to the saloon car, its chard and blackened back still smouldered.

 Moving away, the soldiers wandered around, trying to take in the appalling scene around them. The single-track road was littered with suitcases, shoes, books, bedding, blankets, body parts and corpses. Ugly black crows circled overhead, swooping down and pecking at the dead, squabbling and fighting amongst themselves for the favoured carrion.

 Macbeth flicked the safety off his Enfield and shot a large hog through the head as it fed on the body of an infant. The startled animal rolled over, squealing in its death throes, limbs quivering as it expired. Other hogs fled, grunting their disapproval at being so rudely interrupted during their mealtime, and ran for cover as Macbeth worked the bolt of his Enfield.

The single shot also sent the crows aloft, climbing into the stinking, smoking air. One or two refused to relinquish their spoils and stood their ground until Macbeth shot the biggest one. His black, bloody feathers exploded from his disintegrating body as the .303 round tore through its flesh. The rest seemed to get the message and climbed away. Each soldier surveyed the ghastly surroundings without talking. The pitiful, dead adults were nothing compared to the crumpled, torn bodies of the children and babies, a sight that made nightmares inevitable for them all.

The young men wandered up and down the road, looking for any survivors. In places, they were forced back into the trees to get around enormous bomb craters, so wide and deep that they covered the entire road. Particularly gruesome was the difficulty of avoiding stepping in human and animal remains.

Another shot rang out in the noxious air as Evans despatched an agonised horse. Simms, who had never seen the dead before, retreated into the trees to retch the contents of his stomach out.

Macbeth walked slowly on down the road and shot another hog, who had dared a quick foray on to the road. Chambering another round, he passed broken carts with stiff dead horses still harnessed in their shafts. He skirted around another horse, slipping as he did so on its entrails, which spewed out across the road from its torn belly. A murder of crows perched in their trees watched Macbeth, cawing their irritation, eager to return to their feasting. Another shot rang out further up the road as Evans continued his grisly task.

Simms was feeling a little better now and drank from his water bottle to rid the rancid taste from his mouth. The stench of the place was suffocating him and he didn't want to see anymore of this vile business, so he took himself off to rest under an Oak.

Witherspoon and Boyce appeared out of the trees. Boyce had dark bags under his eyes which accentuated his sunken, hollow cheeks. Simms thought he looked worse than some of the cadavers lying about. Witherspoon helped Boyce settle down next to the ailing Simms and then carried on to find Evans. 'You stink worse than ever, Simmo,' said Boyce.

Simms ignored Boyce. Moisture welled up in his eyes, and the lump grew in his throat as he put his head in his hands to hide his tears.

Evans had gone in the opposite direction to Macbeth. He walked carefully along the road, avoiding body parts and bloody pools.

Among the dead littering the road, he came across a French Army Officer, his vacant eyes staring up at the sky. Evans respectfully removed his belt and took possession of his sidearm, which turned out to be a fine Label revolver. The pistol was in good condition, little used and well oiled. He slipped it back into its holster and tucked it inside his battledress, pleased with his find. He noticed that some horses and other animals had no discernible marks on them at all, while others were mutilated and had suffered horrific wounds. Any injured animals he dispatched quickly with a bullet through the head. The place looked and smelt like an abattoir.

Simms felt the urge to retch coming on again, so he looked around for something to cover his face. Opening a small suitcase, the contents spilled out over the ground. He rummaged through the pile of women's undergarments and toiletries, peeling off the top pair of pink knickers. He noted the very good quality silk. Simms unscrewed the top of a beautiful, ornate bottle of lavender water and liberally sprinkled the contents over the absorbent gusset. Removing his spectacles, he pulled the sweet smelling garment over his head, and positioning the gusset over his nose and mouth and using the leg holes to see out of, he clipped his wire spectacles back over his ears to keep the mask in place. He felt instant relief. Even the flies and midges seem to leave him alone as he lay back and closed his sore eyes.

Boyce, not to miss an opportunity, staggered to his feet and hobbled over to an open suitcase and inspected the contents for valuables. Finding nothing, he peered around, careful not to be seen as he rifled through the pockets of an old man. He found a gold pocket watch attached to a chain. The front glass had a crack in it, but it was of excellent quality and the second hand moved steadily around the face. He moved around gleefully sifting corpses and suitcases, even feeling the linings of coats and jackets for hidden valuables.

Soon he had accumulated a small pile of valuable artefacts that he stowed in his haversack. Boyce caught the unmistakable glint of gold in the mouth of an old woman. As he was prising the gold tooth from of her jaw, he felt he was being watched. Looking around his eye caught sight of a slight movement in a tree, and there, sitting on a branch, watching his every move, was a small brown monkey. He had very large brown eyes compared to his head, which was stressed by dark rings of fur around them, and he seemed curious about Boyce and what he was doing.

The near naked soldier took exception to being spied on and threw a stone at it. The voyeur scampered off up the tree and bounded from branch to branch, screeching and whimpering, before disappearing into the foliage.

'Cheeky bloody monkey.' said Boyce, adjusting his scrotum and slowly squatting down, before resuming his extraction.

Macbeth had now walked down towards the end of this long column of vehicles and carts. The last thing he expected to see was a large grey elephant. It was perfectly still, squat down on its knees, its head braced and supported on its yellow streaked tusks, its corrugated trunk bulged out between them, ending in a bloody mess. Its eyes had been pecked out. Red and white striations ran down from the sockets over its cheeks and its large kite ears hung limp like empty mail sacks.

Macbeth stood before the magnificent beast as tears welled up in his eyes. This was the first elephant he had seen since he was a boy, taken to the circus as a birthday treat by his father. The memory came flooding back to him now, spending time with his father, who died soon after the circus visit, another victim of mustard gas.

The Elephant had been pulling a large, rubber wheeled wagon, brightly painted with the head of a grinning clown emblazoned on the side, with the word 'CIRCUS' above the clown in equally bright colours.

Other Circus vehicles lay abandoned behind. Lorries with cages rented from their flatbed mountings lay among the trees, their occupants long gone. As he moved closer, he could make out the damaged sign bearing the painted figure of a roaring lion. The cage behind had apparently housed Tigers. Macbeth looked nervously around to make sure the occupants were not still around and looking for a short ginger corporal to have for lunch.

An ice cream trike lay upside down, smashed and broken, yellow cones scattered in a small pool of vanilla mush. Hog prints trailed through and away from it.

Witherspoon joined Macbeth, who looked equally disturbed and upset. The two soldiers walked on in silence until, as they rounded a cart, Macbeth stopped and stared at an unexploded bomb, just a few feet away.

'Don't go near it if I were you, corporal,' said Witherspoon.

'I wonder what would happen if I hit it with a hammer,' replied Macbeth, sarcastically, edging round the buckled finned casing. The bomb rested on the ground as if lowered in place by a giant crane, the only evidence of its journey being skid marks on the ground.

'Don't thee joke about the 'orrible looking thing,' said Witherspoon, backing well away.

'Mabey, the trees cushioned its fall,' said Macbeth, examining the unexploded ordnance close up. 'Could be one of those timed buggers, you know, that explode hours later to catch poor devils like us.'

'You a mean it could go off, corp?' Witherspoon asked, backing even further away.

'Only if it's ticking,' replied Macbeth jokingly. He removed his helmet and knelt down beside the bomb, putting his right ear against the casing next to a couple of circular fuse caps.

'Well, I'll be jiggered,' Macbeth moved away from the bomb. 'It's ticking like a grandfather clock.'

'Oh, bugger me.' exclaimed Witherspoon. 'I do believe it's time to move on, corporal.

Let's get away from the dreadful thing.'

The flies were gathering apace in the heat of the day as Boyce went about his larceny. He kept looking over his shoulder to make sure he was not being observed by man or monkey.

Some bodies were so riddled with the black insects that even he bulked at disturbing them and as the morphine was wearing off, his whole groin area felt on fire. He sat down and poured the dregs of his water bottle over his loincloth and felt instant relief. Lighting a cigarette, he exhaled the blue smoke and counted the haul of gold teeth he had removed. The gold felt heavy in his hands and he was well pleased with his dentistry skill.

Looking across the road, he noticed, for the first time, a British Army Bren gun carrier.

The vehicle was wedged up between two trees at a forty-five degree angle. Boyce made his way around the side of the carrier and it seemed undamaged until he found a hole in the engine cover. A large piece of shrapnel had shattered the engine block. Clambering over the bulkhead, he found the driver, dressed in a khaki uniform, slumped over the steering wheel. Boyce relived him of his wristwatch, and pulling the body back off the wheel, he found an almost full packet of players in his tunic pocket.

'You won't be needin' them, pal,' he whispered in the dead man's ear.

He was about to search the back when he heard a groan. Boyce looked again at the dull, clouded eyes of the driver when he heard the groan again. Climbing uncomfortably into the back of the vehicle, he peered over the other side to discover another soldier lying on the ground. The prostrate soldier groaned once more, and his leg moved.

'Bugger it,' said Boyce, taking another drag from his cigarette.

Macbeth took off his helmet and wiped the sweat off his head and the interior leather band of his Brodie helmet, which had been chafing his temples to where blood now clotted in his hair. Looking around, he found a red silk scarf with black dots tangled in the branches of a tree. He wrapped the scarf around his head and tied it off at the back as a bandana. Putting his helmet back on, he made his way back up the reeking road, past the bloated cadavers, to gather his men together.

He came across Simms wearing the pink knickers over his face. As Macbeth was about to speak, the lavender scent caught his nostrils.

'Sorry corp, I can't stand the smell like,' said Simms, lifting the front of his gusset so he could talk.

'Not part of the uniform, Simms.'

'No corp,' replied Simms, noticing the red silk bandana under the corporal's helmet.

'Sort it Simms, sort it.'

'Righto corp.'

As Macbeth stepped out onto the roadway, 'Right you lot, it's time to make tracks. There's a ruddy big bomb about to blow and we need to be far away. Where the hell is Gunga Din? Witherspoon, you were supposed to be watching out for him.'

'I left him over there with Simms, so he could rest awhile.' replied Witherspoon, looking sheepishly around for Boyce.

The call went out, Macbeth shouted his name in the fly infested air and heard a faint shout in return.

'I don't like the thought of levin' the folk unburied corporal. Can anything be done for them?' asked Witherspoon.

'No.' 'Oh,' said Witherspoon, looking despondent. Boyce shouted to the assembly from a hundred yards further up the road to come and see something. Macbeth cursed and stroud off. 'Better be bloody important.'

The others followed the little NCO with Simms, bringing up the rear, wearing his pink knickers, glasses and helmet.

Macbeth found Boyce hanging to the side of the Bren gun carrier.

'We've got a live one here corp.' said Boyce. Macbeth knelt down beside the khaki clad private and felt his pulse. Retrieving his water bottle, he gave the soldier a drink. The young soldier looked up into the eyes of the gathering throng. 'Thanks.' he muttered to Macbeth.

Witherspoon looked the teenage boy over for any wounds or broken bones, but found he was suffering from concussion.

'Christ, he's just left school by the look of him,' said Evans.

'Can he be moved, Witherspoon?' asked Macbeth anxiously.

'Don't know. He could have some internal injuries or the like, corporal.'

'We'll have to take him with us. Can you carry him, Witherspoon?' asked Macbeth. 'We can manage him between us,' said Evans. 'Right then. Let's move out,' ordered Macbeth.

Boyce tugged on Witherspoon's arm and said, 'I need some more painkillers. It's me knackers, 'urtin bad now they are.' Witherspoon gave Boyce half a dose of opiate and offered to carry his knapsack.

'No, that's all right me, 'ol mucker I can take care of it.' Boyce hugged his knapsack, bearing his contraband.

The troop fell in on the road and moved off, glad to be away from the scene of carnage and to breathe fresh but humid air again. When they had covered a mile or so, Macbeth called a halt to allow the men to rest. Evans, who had taken on carrying the injured boy soldier first, laid him down in the shade of an old oak tree. After giving him some water, Evans asked him what his name was and what unit he was with.

The young soldier looked puzzled and said he could remember nothing, including his name. Evans searched his pockets to see if he was carrying anything that could identify him. His battledress bore the insignia of the Royal Artillery.

Macbeth came up to see how the young soldier was doing. Evans explained he was still suffering from shock, but he was a gunner with the Artillery. They were going to make him a sling to sit in from a couple of rifles threaded through a battledress arms. Boyce, who had been lagging, swaggered up and sat down to drink from his water bottle as Macbeth ordered the troop to fall in.

Chapter 4

The young gunner looked up at the smiling face of Witherspoon and felt reassured.

'How are you feeling now, mate?'

'All right, I suppose. Where am I?'

'You be with friends, my boy,' said Witherspoon, holding the boy's hand.

The boy soldier was around eighteen years old, slim and sallow faced. His sandy fine hair cropped close to the scalp made him look even younger. His cobalt eyes gleamed with the exuberance of youth. 'Ask him if he knows where the battalion is?' Macbeth shouted over.

'Give him a chance, he's still in cuckoo land,' replied Evans.

'My name is Witherspoon. You can call me Witherspoon. What is your name?'

The boy, with a look of consternation on his face, replied, 'I still can't remember. How did I get here?'

'Yo've 'ad a bang on the bonce like, so things may be a little confusin' for you lad,' said Witherspoon, moistening a cotton bandage and laid it on the boy's forehead.

'You just take it easy now, and things will come back to ye. We'll soon get you back to our trenches, if we can find them?' Witherspoon gave the boy a wink and nodded towards the corporal.

The boy tried to sit up, but his head went dizzy. In the distance they heard a low rumble as the timer gave out and the ground trembled slightly beneath their feet. A blue, black cloud mushroomed into the sky, erupting from the distant canopy like an uncorked genie. The clockwork mechanism had run down and made the electrical connection, allowing the device to destroy itself.

Macbeth had no idea in which direction to go. He looked around and found an old Oak tree that dominated the local canopy and called Simms over.

'Simmo, just shimmy up there and have a gander at the landscape.

'Me again, I told you I don't do trees or high things.'

'Look, just shift yourself.'

'Is that an order corp.?'

'Yes.' said Macbeth, taking a drink from his water bottle. 'See if you can spot any water nearby.'

'If it's an order, then,' mumbled Simms as he stomped off, looking to the others for support, which never came. He stripped down to his trousers and pulled his knickers up to his forehead. He stood at the bottom of the tree, looked up and sighed.

Evans stepped up and provided the hand up, pushing at Simms's boots to get him on to the lower branches. From there Simms climbed up each branch, circling around the trunk like a spiral staircase, until he was halfway up. Trying his best not to look down. He looked down and started to panic.

'Bloody high, this is,' Simms bellowed out, clinging to the main trunk like a stick insect.

'Your only ten feet off the ground, Simms, for Christ's sake, get a grip,' shouted Macbeth. Taking off his helmet, he peeled off his bandana and sat in the shade to watch Simms's progress.

'Get a move on Simms, we haven't got all day.' boomed Macbeth.

'Can't,' replied Simms, now fixed on the trunk like a limpet.

'Christ all bloody mighty, I can almost touch your foot from here.' said Macbeth.

'Try to relax there, Simmo,' encouraged Witherspoon. 'Breathe deeply with your peepers shut down. Take al' tensioning out of body and you'll be right as rain.'

Simms did as he was instructed and felt more confident. Opening his eyes, he looked at the rough bark. Little insects dived in and out of the crevices as Simms moved up the tree.

'Remember, move one hand or foot at a time, and make sure that you are secure before moving on,' shouted Evans.

'Come up and show me.' replied Simms.

Macbeth coxed him up to a thick branch halfway up, whereupon Simms refused to go any further. He sat on the branch and steadied himself with a couple of smaller branches and made himself as comfortable as possible in the circumstances. Snapping off some thin branches that obscured his view, he let them drop to the ground.

'Watch what you're doing up there, Simms,' bellowed Macbeth, flinging away the branches that had landed on his head.

'Can't see much.'

'Not again,' mumbled Macbeth.

'Just trees as far as the eye can see.'

'Any sign of water, Simms?'
'No.'

'Anything at all?' shouted Macbeth.

'No.'

'Must be something.'

'Half a mo,' Simms moved a branch aside.

'What is it?'

'There's a nest up here with four eggs in it.' Witherspoon became interested and asked, 'what kind are they Simmo?' 'I think it's a wood pigeon, by the look of it,' came a voice out of the tree.

Macbeth exasperated. 'When you bird watchers have finished, can we get on? Go further up Simms, that's an order.' After a few minutes of cursing and bits of tree falling out of the Oak, Simms had made his way further up the tree and now had a better view of their surroundings.

Macbeth looked forlornly up into the tree. Simms had completely disappeared. 'Where the hell are you?' shouted Macbeth. 'I can see some smoke, corp,' replied Simms. 'We can all see the bleedin smoke from down here Simms, ' said Macbeth, adjusting his sweating crotch area.

'This is from a chimney,' came the disembodied reply. 'Are you sure?' 'I'm pretty sure, over to the West. Couldn't see it before, but it looks like a brick built chimney poking through the tree line.'

'How far?'

'Half a mile at most.'

'Right, well done Simms. Get yourself down now and the rest of you make ready to march.' They lifted the boy on to the makeshift stretcher as the soldiers made ready to move out. Simms descended the Oak and jumped down from the lower branch. Macbeth led the way West. They moved out in single file, Boyce tagged on at the end, still cradling his precious Thompson, his swag bag hanging from his shoulder, humming a salubrious tune to himself.

The phalanx made their way into the darkening forest as a strange howling sound came drifting across the forest fostering deep anxieties in the soldiers as they marched through the never ending trees, high branches closed in on them cutting down the light, so impregnable in places that it appeared night time.

Macbeth slowed a little as he sensed rather than saw a clearing ahead. The smell of wood smoke came drifting over a well-trodden path that led through the trees straight to a little timber framed cottage, nestled in the middle of a glade.

The soldiers gathered up at the tree line to observe. They set the young gunner down as the tired men slumped down on the ground. All seemed quiet. The cottage had been built of stone with a red brick chimney that ran up the gable end, topped off with a terracotta chimney pot and cowl. Another smaller chimney, topped with a cast iron cowl, breached the slate roof to the other side. Thin white smoke crawled out of the cowl and crept around the side wall to vaporise in the humid air.

The youth looked around at the strangers before him and found Boyce staring at him. Boyce gesticulated by crossing a filthy finger across his neck from ear to ear, and then winked.

There was no sign of life from the cottage, and apart from the smoke emanating from the chimney, it looked deserted. There was, however, a line of washing hanging in a picket fence garden to the side, half laid to lawn, the other half given over to vegetables. Beside the front door was a Byre and a lean-to half filled with firewood.

'What do you reckon, then?' Macbeth whispered to Evans over his shoulder.

'Looks quiet enough.'

'Could be a trap.' said Witherspoon 'Could be anything,' replied Evans. 'Well, what do you reckon, then?' Macbeth asked again.

Simms crept forward to whisper, 'This might be where the Jerry signals are coming from corp.'

Just as Macbeth's brain was still analysing the information, an old man came out the front door and walked over to the washing line. He took down a large white bed sheet and went back inside.

'Who the hell is that, geezer?' ventured Boyce.

'I was a thinkin' that we should knock on the door like, and ask for some water from the old man,' said Witherspoon.

'He could be fifth column and rat us in.' hissed Macbeth. 'Looks like a Woodman's gaff to me,' said Evans

'Lovely garden though, veg and fruit trees.' said Witherspoon.

'He's probably a bloody spy, you know, one of them filthy column geezers,' pointed out Boyce. 'Fifth column,' corrected Evans.

'The place could be heaving with the bloody SS, for all we know,' said Simms, smirking.

'Oh,' said Witherspoon, 'I don't like the sound of that.'

'Let me go in corp.,' Boyce ventured, 'I'll sort the bugger out, lob a grenade through one of the windows and …'

'Stow it, Boyce,' said Macbeth. 'Could this be where the signals are coming from Simms?'

Simms turned on the RT set and waited for the tubes to warm up. The static started in crackling and whistling. Simms turned the tuning knob until the morse signals came over so loud that Simms moved the earphone away.

'If he's not in the cottage, he must be within a couple of hundred yards of us.' said Simms.

'What do you reckon, Evans?' asked Macbeth, not sure of anything.

The front door opened again and the thin man emerged carrying a small, cheaply made suitcase. He was dressed in a black suit, black work boots. and carried the suitcase carefully, keeping it horizontal and not by its handle. As the soldiers looked on, the man made his way into the garden and, passing under the line of washing, he disappeared out of sight. Macbeth was just about to ask Evans what he thought when the man reappeared and entered the Byre next to the lean to. He came out carrying a shovel.

'What's the bugger up to?' mumbled Macbeth. 'Dunno, ' said Evans.

'Do you reckon he looks kosher?' asked Macbeth, looking at Evans.

'He's fuckin filth column,' croaked Boyce from the back.

'Simms, nip round the other side and see what he's doing.' ordered Macbeth.

'Why have I got to go?' protested Simms.

'I'll go, for fuck's sake, this is not a bloody scout troop.' said Evans. Picking up his Enfield he skirted back into the trees and made his way around the side.

Macbeth gave Simms a scolding look and said, 'That's what happens when you don't obey orders. Evans has gone off in a huff now.

Just bloody do what you 're told for Christ's sake.'

'You don't want to take the Lord's name in vain, you don't,' said Witherspoon. 'Just fucking zip it Witherspoon,' snarled Macbeth. Simms turned the RT off and packed it away. Just as he turned to pick up his rifle he caught sight of Boyce spread eagled laying on the grass. He had removed his loincloth and was applying a libation of gun oil to his crotch area. His bald, multi coloured penis and scutum glistened in the afternoon sun.

Evans slipped out of the tree line and, keeping low to the ground, did a monkey crawl around the edge of the picket fence. He peered over the fence to observe the old man digging a hole in the garden. Evans made his way back to report.

'What's he digging a hole for?' asked Macbeth. 'How should I know?' replied Evans.

'Fat good you are.'

'He's digging a bloody hole, you said go and….'

'Shut it. He must be digging a hole for a reason, that's what you were supposed to find out.'

'He's a fuckin' Nazi geezer, let me sort him out corp,' said Boyce.

'I don't think you should jump to judge the man so,' said Witherspoon indignantly. 'he may be a plantin' another fruit tree or summat.'

The boy gunner sat watching and listening to this band of loons, totally confused. Feeling he was still in some sort of dreamland, he drank some water and poured the rest over his head. He looked over at Boyce, the self mutilator, sunning his glistening genitalia.

If he ever was to make his way out of this forest and get back home, he would be better off on his own. He found the experience depressing, and his head thumped inside like a timpani drum. Lying back down, he replaced the damp flannel on his forehead, and closing his eyes, he tried to doze. 'Plant a tree?' Macbeth held his head in his hands.

'He could be planting a tree. If he's a Woodsman, that's the sort of thing they do,' said Witherspoon.

'He's a bloody racist. I'll bet he's the one who's sending the bloody coded messages over the radio, ' croaked Boyce. 'You mean Fascist, Boyce' corrected Simms. 'Bastard, it's probably the very radio he is burying to keep it hidden,' said Boyce as he picked dead flies off his lower belly and crotch.

All the soldiers went silent for a moment and looked at Boyce.

'Bollock brain could have a point there, corp,' said Evans.

'You just said you didn't know,' said Macbeth, getting confused.

'We need to see what's in the case. If he's hiding it, why is he hiding it.'' replied Evans 'He did look agitated, sort of furtive, like,' said Simms, trying to be helpful.

Macbeth, exasperated, ordered an orderly withdrawal to the other side of the cottage. They left the boy to rest. They made there way around the tree line.

The troop collectively peered through the picket fence like naughty boys out for a days scrumping.

The old man had removed his suit jacket and was lifting the small suitcase and carefully placed it in the hole.

'Why is he burying a suitcase?' Macbeth whispered to no one in particular.

'That will be his bloody transmitter,' said

Boyce. 'I said that geezer was a columnist.' You can't just go accusing the chap of being a spy and all, you'll all going off 'alf cocked, like a load of bleedin' idiots, you are,' said Witherspoon.

'Then what's in the suitcase then? And why is he burying it in the ground,' asked Macbeth?

Witherspoon looked around at his comrades. 'Well, I don't know that, do I.'

'Just plug the fucker and have done with it.' whispered Boyce, who had crept up the fence and knelt next to Macbeth. The corporal inched away after inhaling the rotting stench emanating from Boyce's groin area. 'Shut up Boyce, I need to think on this one.'' said Macbeth wrapping his bandana around over his nose and mouth. As he tied the knot, Evans vaulted over the fence, pointed his Enfield at the old man and ordered him to surrender.

The old, thin man held his arms in the air. His trousers were held up with braces, the waist just under his armpits. He stood before them, his sallow face wore the mask of sadness, his lacklustre eyes filled with tears.

Boyce winced as he tried to climb over the pointed picket fence. Catching his loincloth on a projecting nail, he lost his balance and spun headlong into a fresh pile of manure.

Macbeth had also miscalculated the height of the fence and found he could not negotiate it. He plumped to go around to the side to find something to stand on. By the time he had found an old upturned wheelbarrow and cleared the fence, a shot rang out and the old man lay dead on the ground, blood oozing from his left eye socket.

'What the hell happened there?' asked Macbeth.

'He went for me corp, as I tried to look in the case, he just came at me.' Evans replied looking as stunned as Macbeth.

'Just came at me nothing I could do, just came on.'

'Alright, the deed is done now. Simms open the bleedin case. Witherspoon go through his pockets.' Ordered Macbeth.

'Right you are, corporal, but seems a shame to shoot the man like that,' said Witherspoon, shouldering his Enfield. He patted the man's pockets and picked up his jacket, felt inside and found nothing.

'I told you, he just came at me. I didn't mean to kill the old man.' Evans looked ashamed and wandered off. Boyce hobbled up, scraping bits of manure off his legs and chest, which had stuck to the gun oil.

Simms bent down next to the hole and lifted the small case out and placed it on the ground. Gingerly, he lifted the lid a little and checked for any booby trap wires. The other soldiers, sensing a possible explosion, moved back. Simms hesitated slightly before lifting the lid up sufficiently to peer inside. Seeing no wires or anything suspicious, he lifted the lid fully open. Packed tightly inside was a white silk shawl. As Simms began to unwrap the folds of the shawl, he looked upon the face of a new born baby.

Macbeth gave out a sort of choked sound as he saw the infant's face. Simms wrapped the blanket back up and closed the lid.

The boy gunner, finding himself abandoned, walked unsteadily over to the cottage and made his way to the garden. He found Evans and Witherspoon digging a large hole. He then saw the dead man with the back of his head missing and felt queasy. His headache came back, and he was feeling giddy.

Simms helped him to a garden bench, where he sat down and had a drink of water. Simms filled him in on recent events. He told him that Evans had also found the dead body of a woman upstairs. The sheets were covered in blood and he thinks she died from birthing the still-born baby.

Evans wants to place all the bodies in the cottage and burn it, to cremate the whole family together. Macbeth would not have it, he said it would alert any Jerries in the area. The boy noticed that Simms's voice was breaking up and his eyes were filling. The sound of shovels came to an end. Witherspoon and Evans moved over to the skinny cadaver. The two men lifted the body with hardly any effort at all and respectfully placed him in the freshly dug grave. Macbeth emerged from the cottage, carrying the dead woman wrapped in the bloodstained sheets. He placed her next to the old man, Witherspoon followed, carrying the small suitcase, and placed it at the feet of the two bodies.

Macbeth gathered the soldiers to the graveside. They all removed their helmets and stood looking at the bodies. 'Does anyone want to say any words before we cover them up?' asked Macbeth.

The rest looked uneasy and glanced at each other, hoping that someone else would step up. In the end, it was Witherspoon that broke the silence.

'I would just like to say that although we did not know these poor folks, I would like to think that they were good Christian people and did the best they could. I don't know much about the holy ghost and that but, whatever there god should be I hope he's watching over them right now.' Witherspoon then made the sign of the cross, even though he was not a catholic, he thought the situation warranted it. Macbeth looked up and taking up a handful of soil threw it into the grave. 'Well said Private.' As he moved off, the other soldiers took up some soil and mumbled something before dropping it into the grave.

The sound of shovels started again as the flies gathered and darted around their heads. Macbeth decided the men could do with a brew and sent Simms to reccy the kitchen for a kettle. The range was already fired up and as he went to fill the kettle with fresh water, he was startled by a small monkey standing in the doorway. Simms stood still and just looked at the small animal. The monkey stared back at Simms with his large brown eyes. Simms looked around the kitchen and found some stale bread. He offered the bread to the primate, who snatched the offering and ran outside and hid under a small shrubbery.

The little corporal entered the cottage and found the interior was dark and smelled musty. He stood still for a few moments, just inside the front door to allow his eyes to adjust before moving across the flagstone floor. In front of him he found a large brick built fireplace, a raised stone hearth protruded out into the gloomy room, with fixed iron brackets built in to the mortar courses. To the left-hand side of the main fireplace was a cast iron oven with a well-worn door and catch. Oak beams crisscrossed the low ceiling from front to back, to which small brass objects had been nailed. The glass in the softwood casement windows looked opaque with years of accumulated grime.

 A narrow staircase framed the opposite wall leading to the attic rooms above. The cottage was devoid of any soft furnishings, carpets, or curtains. The sparse furniture, dining table, chairs and benches, had been crudely fashioned from old barrels and sawed timber.

 Macbeth could hear Boyce walking about on the floor above as he moved around in his hobnailed boots, opening and shutting cupboard doors. The little corporal crossed the living room to the only other door, which led into the kitchen. On opening the door, he saw Simms standing in the doorway, looking out into the garden.

 'Where's this tea then, Simms?'

 'I just saw a Monkey run out into the garden.' replied Simms, still holding the empty kettle in his hand. Macbeth had always harboured doubts about Simms.

 'That kettle will not boil in your hand, Private.' Simms hung the kettle from the hand pumped tap and worked the lever. After some gurgling sounds, the water gushed from the nozzle and filled the kettle. He replaced the lid and set it on the range to boil. The kitchen, with the heat from the range, was stifling, so Simms went back outside into the garden. He looked under the shrubbery to see if the monkey was still there, but there was no sign of him.

Boyce was going through the cottage to find anything that might prove useful or valuable. The cottage had only two rooms in the attic and was as sparsely furnished as the ground floor. There was little to find. The couple proved to be living hand to mouth with very little comforts or family heirlooms ferreted away. Boyce, empty-handed, went outside to the garden to find the others resting in the shade of an old apple tree. He was surprised to see Witherspoon cuddling a small monkey.

It looked familiar.

The little monkey clung to the big man as if his life depended on it. Witherspoon reciprocated by feeding the little fellow titbits every so often and gave an irrepressible grin of satisfaction that he had gained a new friend. As he waited for the kettle to boil, Simms set up the RT on a low wall that ran outside the kitchen wall, down to the picket fence. Even without putting on the earphones, he could hear the distinctive Morse coming over loud and clear again. He was certain that the operator was close by. Simms could only find an old, well-used saucepan with an ill-fitting lid to brew the tea in, and after warming the pan he measured out one teaspoon of loose tea leaves per person and one for the pot.

Pouring the boiling water over the leaves, he then stirred the browning brew with a wooden spoon, first clockwise and then anticlockwise, before covering the infusion. He then gathered together the chipped enamel mugs and cleaned each in turn, except the one he had reserved for Boyce, as this mug was not only the dirtiest but also had a split in the bottom which allowed the contents to weep out.

Finding a unexpected small quantity of sugar in one cupboard, hidden away in the living room, he added a little extra to Macbeth's mug, as he knew the corporal had a sweet tooth. As he was about to go back into the kitchen a movement caught his eye. He strained to see through the opaque glass, where the movement had occurred, but it was so caked he had to apply water to a piece of cloth and rub a small circle clean before he could peer out.

Emerging from the tree line, he saw a group of German soldiers walking towards the

cottage. 'Jesus.'

Simms bolted for the garden door, tripping over a chair that Boyce had left on the floor, causing him to land heavily on the flags and winding himself. He lay prostrate on the floor, unable to breathe, panic erupting inside his head as he struggled to suck in the vital oxygen. Seconds ticked away as he gasped for air, seeing in his mind's eye the enemy soldiers approaching outside, anticipating the sound of gunfire and shouting at any moment. He managed to roll over and crawled to the open door.

'Where's the bleedin tea then?' Macbeth demanded as Simms came out the doorway on his hands and knees.

Simms dragged himself out and spluttered incoherently, 'Jerries on the other side.' 'What did he say?' asked Macbeth.

'Sounded like berries in pies,' replied Witherspoon.

Simms took in a lungful of air and shouted,

'Fucking Jerries are here.'

'Shit, how many?'

'Dozen, at least.'

The soldiers moved as one entity. Packs and rifles were grabbed, the troop headed down the garden, past the grave and made for the tree line. Simms helped the boy along and

Witherspoon, clutching the monkey, ran ahead, passing Macbeth. Trying to keep the cottage between them and the approaching soldiers, the troop ran as fast as they could across the open ground, glancing over their shoulders as they fled.

Evans, who had been caught with his boots off, was the last away and sprinted over the rough ground with his lace less boots flopping around on his feet. Even with this handicap he caught up with Boyce, who was running like a penguin, cursing, trying to balance his pack and Thompson. His loincloth was slipping down and hung like a clocks pendulum. As he passed him he shouted, 'run you lazy bugger!'

'Fuck off'

Witherspoon loped across the open ground, the little monkey, frightened and scared, leapt off his back pack and hid behind a small bush. The big man made the tree line first. Simms and the Gunner ran in a sort of zigzag pattern, that Simms had seen in a training film once.

A single rifle shot eventually broke the peace, signalling to the fleeing British soldiers that they had been spotted. This was quickly followed by other rifle reports and short bursts of automatic fire, which eerily echoed off the trees that they were running towards. Witherspoon returned the fire, working the bolt on his Enfield as fast as he could. A bullet sounding like an insect buzz went past Macbeth's ear. His little legs doubled their pace as his lungs felt they were going to burst. He seemed to be covering the ground in slow motion, every muscle in his body screamed to rest and the tree line seemed so far away, and yet he knew it was only a matter of yards.

Witherspoon kept up a good rate of fire, trying to keep the Jerries heads down. Evans reached the tree line and immediately began to fire his rifle in support. Macbeth eventually made the trees and dived for cover, closely followed by Simms. Boyce was the only target left in the open as he hobbled and dodged and weaved his way across the uneven ground. His loincloth had now fallen down around his ankles but he still managed to keep forward movement.

Pieces of bark splintered off the tree over Evan's head. The German soldiers had fanned out and were difficult to locate. Macbeth and his troop just fired at the rifle flashes and hoped to keep their aim off. Boyce eventually made the tree line and collapsed among the ferns. He grabbed his Thomson and fired short bursts back at his assailants.

Evans worked the bolt of his Enfield like a watch maker, taking his time now that he had calmed down, he took careful aim before firing. He saw several enemy soldiers drop.

Boyce now spotted the little brown monkey shaking behind a bush. He took careful aim and fired a short burst. The primate flew into the air, as if lifted by an invisible hand and landed some feet away, quivering.

The enemy stopped firing, and all went suddenly quiet. Macbeth was watching the open ground and could see the enemy soldiers trying to work their way around the sides, using the trees and ferns as cover.

'The buggers are trying to outflank us, a pincer movement' said Macbeth,'

Witherspoon and Evans smiled at each other. Macbeth now spotted a German soldier, who, for some reason or another, just stood up in full view, and moved from cover to cover. Macbeth lifted his Enfield and sighted on the soldier as he left cover. He squeezed the trigger and felt the butt kick. The German soldier seemed to stand still for a moment, almost surprised at receiving a bullet in the middle of his chest. He looked down at the bloody hole before falling forwards on his face in the dirt.

Macbeth gave the order to move out. Evans stayed behind and gave covering fire with Boyce's Thompson. The troop moved off as fast as they could. Witherspoon put Boyce over his shoulder and carried him in a fireman's lift to make better time.

Simms, now without the weight of the RT, helped the boy navigate their way through the trees.

Evans changed magazines on the Thompson, gave another couple of bursts before following the others through the trees. The troop disappeared like phantoms. After sometime Macbeth called a halt and the men collapsed as one on the ground breathing heavily. Witherspoon laid Boyce out and gave him some water. All water bottles were being opened and drained.

Evans came up and reported that the enemy were not in pursuit. Holding his water bottle, he found himself shaking as the adrenalin started to subside.

'Well, we can't stay here men, we have to move out.' Macbeth said as he stood up and slung his backpack on and checked his Enfield, slipping the safety on. One by one, the tired and exhausted soldiers stood up and readied themselves. Macbeth led the way and soon came across a trackway. He looked up and down the empty road and plumped on the direction that gave the most shade, and the track sloped downhill. He hoped the track would lead to a stream or river. Boyce waddled along the path with his pack. His loincloth had fallen off during the escape and the damp, filthy vest hanging down to his knees looked more like a dress. His black hobnailed boots felt like lead weights. Evans handed him his Tommy gun and spare drums. 'You could have cleaned it, Evans, ' Boyce said with a stupid grin on his face.

Evans ignored the comment and walked on.

'Turd eater.'

Evans turned around and came trotting back. Boyce stopped in his tracks and hobbled off into the trees to hide. He crouched down among the ferns and kept perfectly still. Evans came through the gap that Boyce had used and stood still, waiting for Boyce to give his position away. He stood on a small twig which cracked like a rifle going off. With a lightning flash, Evans had his hand around Boyce's throat. 'I'm going to squeeze your little, black bollocks, Boyce,' said Evans, then went on. 'I've got a nice big present here for you it will fit nicely up your rear end.' 'Sorry Evans, didn't mean it, honest,' grovelled Boyce.

'I saw what you did back there, to Witherspoon's monkey, you little shit.'

'Don't tell 'im will you?

'I might do if you fuck me about again.' 'Sorry Evans, I won't do it again, promise.' pleaded Boyce, finding it hard to breathe. 'You call me that again sunshine and I'll toast your feet in a fire, got it.'

'I got it,' croaked Boyce, red faced. Evans let Boyce go, as the stench was getting unbearable. His reeking vest had caught on a branch, exposing his fetid cock. Evans felt his stomach turn and moved away quickly. Boyce collapsed to the ground and held his neck, taking deep breaths, and watched as Evans marched away.

'Fucking Turd eater,' he croaked.

Chapter 5

The fatigued soldiers had covered another mile or so and then stopped for a rest. A mist had settled up to around knee height, which made them look as if they were levitating. With water bottles empty, the men were getting desperate. When Boyce caught up with the troop, each of the sweating, inanimate figures had a cloud of midges hovering around them, like a spiritual aura. Macbeth sat on a tree stump, looking like a little garden gnome, stripped to the waist he was attempting to wipe himself down with a brown rag. The midges seemed to have got bigger somehow and came in to attack his delicate white skin in a coordinated formation. He swiped at them with his rag and cursed the humid heat. 'Has anyone seen my little monkey?' asked Witherspoon. Boyce, looking red faced, looked over at Evans who said nothing.

'Fuck the bloody monkey,' said Macbeth, irritated. As he looked upon the men under his command, he felt relief that he had at least not lost anyone in the recent fracas. The affair could have been nasty, and they must find water soon. He looked over at Simms, stretched out on the verge and barked an order,

'Simms, get on the set and see if there's any news,' Simms sat up and drank the last dregs from his water bottle. Rousing himself, he crawled on all fours over to his pack and realised that he had left the radio back in the kitchen.

'Shit,' Simms braced himself as the words came out, 'Corp, you'll never guess, where the radio is?'

Macbeth looked up and spat a dead fly from his salty lips, 'What?'

'I left the RT back in the cottage.' 'Don't piss me about Simms,'

'Wasn't my fault, it was the bloody Germans turning up and all.'

'You've lost the radio,' Macbeth put his head in his hands and mumbled,

'I don't believe it, our only way of finding out what's going on and you lose it.'

'Sorry, I suppose it was a gut reaction to warn you chaps.' Macbeth lifted his head from his hands and glared at Simms.

'Sorry, you were in charge of the bloody radio laddie, it was your responsibility,' Macbeth pointed an accusing finger at Simms.

'This bickering is getting us nowhere. The damn radio is gone, so let's just get used to it,' said Evans.

'You're a bloody disgrace, Simms.' Macbeth had to have the last word.

Boyce grinned at Simms and carried on picking at a scab on his leg.

'Never mind, let's just get away from here,' said Evans, getting to his feet and grabbing his rifle.

Macbeth stood up with a look of determination on his red face, 'We'll have to go back for it.'

There was silence. The birds seem to sing in harmony all around them as each man looked from one to the other. Evans eventually asked, 'What was that?'

'We've got to get that radio back. It's our only lifeline, don't you see? Without it we are just blind mice, running around in the dark, going in circles.' Macbeth had decided. 'What mice?' piped Boyce.

'The Germans have probably found it by now and either taken it or destroyed it,' said Evans. 'We'll have to take that chance,' anyway if they have scarpered we can fill our water bottles.' Evans conceded the point. As his water bottle was almost exhausted, he knew they had to find water soon.

Macbeth stood up and he quietly readied himself, and the others reluctantly followed suit. The promise of water seemed to overcome the danger they may face if the enemy was still there. No one questioned his order as they set out to retrace their steps back to the cottage. The men moved out silently, the mood turning black as anxiety set in.   Simms was assigned to bring up the rear, which he was glad to do after the nasty looks he received from his comrades. He kept well back, trailing along, thankful not to have to talk to anyone.

Boyce, making sure that Simms was watching, dropped his loincloth and wriggled his bare red arse at him. Simms ignored the fool and pretended that he hadn't noticed. Boyce then produced his thick rubber band and fired an acorn at him. Which, because of the sheer accuracy of the shot, Simms was obliged to duck. Boyce grinned and gave him the archer's salute as he waddled on to catch up with the others. Every so often he stopped, bared his bony buttocks and let wind.

As they made their way back towards the cottage, a strange sound came to them over the stilted air, a sound that was not of the wood. A howling, screeching sound that had enough resonance to carry it over a great distance. A sound that halted the troop in their tracks and sent shivers racing through backbones. The men looked at each other and listened. The sound had gone as quickly as it had come. Macbeth broke the silence when he ordered Evans to scout ahead, as they were now only a quarter of a mile from the cottage. Even the flies had abandoned them to their fate. Evans moved off and Macbeth called a halt and rest.   He paced up and down the track, waiting anxiously for Evans to return. Witherspoon helped the youth to lie in some shade and gave him the remnants of his water bottle. The young man thanked him and instantly fell into a deep sleep. Witherspoon found a tree he could lean against and, after removing his helmet, mopped his brow and dosed. After a while, Macbeth could see Evans returning, making his way up the track, keeping close to the verge ferns.

'Nazi fucks are digging graves corp.'

'Any sentries out?'

'No.'

'How many of them?'

'I counted ten, but there could be more,' said Evans.

'Alright, ten you say, two to one, well we'll keep an eye on them for now,' said Macbeth.

Witherspoon reluctantly woke the boy. He stood and stretched and fell in with the others. As the troop approached the cottage, Macbeth put his finger up to his mouth to warn everyone to keep quiet.

Evans led the way through the trees to a spot where there was still sufficient cover for the men to observe the cottage without being seen. Macbeth positioned the men behind a fallen tree on the edge of a tree line. The cottage was framed in sunshine, a few hundred yards away across the cleared ground. Evans and Macbeth made their way to the thick end of the fallen tree and crouched down among the spindly founds of the root tendrils, covered in clumps of reddish clay. The two soldiers made themselves as comfortable as they could before Macbeth removed his soaking red bandana and squeezed the moisture out.

They had an unobstructed view of the German soldiers, who were hard at work digging graves for their fallen comrades in the vegetable garden. As they watched, the enemy dig, stripped, sweating and glistening in the sun. The odd carrot and swede came out to be placed neatly to the side.

Several Germans were lazing around the front door drinking something hot from white enamel mugs.

'Bloody cheek, they're drinking our tea,' remarked Macbeth scornfully.

'Just do with a cuppa,' answered Evans, licking his salty lips. 'Reckon we could take them?' asked Macbeth

Evans looked back at the men gathered and resting behind the fallen tree, and then back at Macbeth. Evans reckoned they had five active soldiers, with four rifles and one submachine gun. 'Not a hope in hell'.

The two men watched as the enemy soldiers laid the cadavers, wrapped in white bedsheets, on the ground next to the graves that were being dug.

Macbeth summoned Simms to come up to the root end. 'They are all busy at the mo burying their dead. Do you reckon you can nip in and get the RT from the kitchen without being seen?'

Simms looked over at the scene in the vegetable garden and scratched his head.

'Dunno corp, l suppose I could have a bash.'

Simms slid off his backpack and, taking up his rifle, he made to go when Evans held his arm. 'Leave the rifle Simmo, better take this', Evans handed over the French revolver.

Simms thanked Evans for the smaller weapon, which would of more use in a confined space than trying to weald a rifle. He made his way along the tree line to emerge from the trees on the opposite side. Crouching low and moving fast, his heart began to beat like thunder. Simms thought he might die before reaching the cottage wall. Suddenly he was at the wall and collapsed in the shaded part under the kitchen window. His hair wet with sweat, he wiped his face and waited for his racing heart to subside. Rising very slowly, he peeked through the semi-obscure glass and could see that the RT was not there. Simms started to panic, and his mind went blank. Sitting back down in the shade, he took a deep breath and contemplated his options. He made his way along the cottage wall and then along the low garden wall to the corner. Evans spotted Simms's head protruding from behind the garden wall first.

'Corp look, there's Simmo, at the corner of the wall.' Macbeth craned his spiky head to see Simms gesturing to them.

'What the hell does he want now?' whispered Macbeth. Evans looked on as Simms glanced over the wall at the gathering Soldiers in the garden and then started to fire an imaginary sub-machine gun.

'He wants the Thompson corp, he must think there's a chance to get them all in one spot.' Evans grabbed the Thomson and some spare magazines from a dozing Boyce and made his way along the tree line, keeping low he followed the same route as Simms and soon got the Kitchen wall. Simms came up to meet him.

'The radios not in the kitchen and we need to get to that water pump.' whispered Simms. Evans checked the Thompson and made his way around the cottage to enter through the front door. He stopped and listened. The cottage was quiet, apart from the voices outside. At the entrance to the kitchen, he halted and peered out into the garden. The corpses had been lowered, and they were gathering at the graveside to say their last words to their fallen comrades.

Evans stepped out from the doorway. With short, accurate busts, he pumped bullets into the backs, bellies, arms, legs, and heads of the startled mourners.

As Evans eased off the trigger, the machine gun barrel gave off a blue acrid smoke. He felt a buzz past his ear and then the report of a rifle crack. As he turned he saw a soldier leaning out of a bedroom window, working the bolt of his Mauser. Macbeth and the rest of the troop opened up from behind the tree, shattering the glass and splintering the wooden frame.

Evans moved back into the kitchen and as he made his way to the living room, he could hear the thump of leather boots coming down the stairwell, he braced himself against the kitchen doorframe and waited for the soldier to reach the top of the stair, his sub-machine gun cocked and ready.

A stick grenade came down the stairwell and bounced off the wall, rolled across the floor and came to a stop in the middle of the room. Evans fired a quick burst through the stairwell wall before diving into the kitchen. A shower of plaster and smoke followed the dull thud of the grenade exploding. Simms came in through the garden door and fired the revolver rapidly at shadowy figures moving from the stairwell. Evans crouched down and fired short bursts into the room, someone screamed and then all went silent.

Macbeth entered the cottage cautiously, stepping over a dead body lying at the foot of the stairwell. He ordered Boyce to check the upper floor before moving to the kitchen to join Evan's and Simms who were busy working the pump and gulping down the clean fresh water. Witherspoon came in, followed by the gunner, and they waited their turn at the pump.

'I've got another fucker up here, corp,' shouted Boyce. Macbeth took a deep drink of the water and replied, 'Bring him down here and make sure he's not armed or hiding anything'

Boyce brought his prisoner down the stairs at rifle point. 'Talk about pen and ink corp. I fink this bugger smells worse than Nazi fucks outside.'

The prisoner came down the stairwell wearing a greatcoat and wellington boots.

'Kamerad'

'Oh no, not you again,' said Macbeth, 'Did you strip search him, Boyce?'

'Give it up corp, I'm doin me best not to throw up er.'

'Go and run him a nice hot bath Boyce, and wash him down,' ordered Macbeth. Boyce, looking bewildered, stared at Macbeth until the corporal smiled at him. 'Leave it out corp, you 'avin me on,' chuckled Boyce. 'Take him outside and get him to backfill the graves. Evans, can you dump the fresh bodies in the graves as well. Save digging any more.' Evans was twenty years old and always avoided looking at the faces of the soldiers, the eyes looking at you, accusingly. It was the faces that you remember. It was the faces that kept you up at night and visit you at quiet moments.

He searched the pockets of the young soldiers, mostly teenagers, and came across the usual photographs of their families, wives, mothers and fathers, sons and daughters. The creased black and white snaps, dog-eared from over handling. Finding nothing of importance, he rolled the bodies in so that there were four corpses in each grave. The last body in was only a foot below the surface.   Evans felt in his pocket and pulled out a packet of Woodbinds. Extracting a near complete cigarette, he lit it and handed it to the German.

The German soldier took the cigarette with a beaming smile on his filthy face and as he said 'Danka' his head exploded inside his helmet.

The soldiers fell to the floor. The loud report and billowing white smoke gave away the enemy position on the tree line. Another burst of smoke and report followed with the round embedding itself in the cottage wall.

Evans grabbed the Thompson and returned fire, giving the tree line some short bursts. The rest of the troop crawled out of the kitchen door and took up positions behind the garden wall. Simms had made his way up the stairs and was firing his Enfield from the bedroom window.

Macbeth shouted up to Simms. 'Can you make out how many are there?'

The firing had stopped, and an eerie silence descended over the farm. The young gunner put his head up above the wall to get a better look.

'Get your head down you dozy bugger' shouted Macbeth. 'I think they scarpered corp,' said Simms.

'Evans, you work your way around to the left. Witherspoon, you go round to the right.'

'It sounds like a pincer movement, corporal,' said Evans.

'No, this is completely different, Evans. When you get to command men, you will find out,' replied Macbeth, his face turning red.

'Well, off you go then,' commanded Macbeth.

Evans and Witherspoon made their way around the tree line while Macbeth and the others were poised to give covering fire if needed. Simms could just make out a body on the ground and remained still as Evans approached. Macbeth peered over the wall as Evans gave the all clear signal.

Witherspoon appeared from the trees to see Evans examining an old musket. At his feet lay the body of a soldier dressed in a French Napoleonic uniform. There was another body a few yards away, also dressed in a similar uniform, a dark blue jacket over a white vest and Shako headgear. Evans turned to Witherspoon.

'What do you make of this, then?' Witherspoon bent down and checked for vital signs, but there were none. He picked up the Shako and looked at the crowned eagle emblem.

'Must be some fancy dress goings on. I'll be reckoned. Might queer though you, might queer,' said Witherspoon wistfully.

'Why would they shoot at us, the frogs are on our side?

Anyway, why use these old muskets?' 'I dunno, I'm sure, might queer.'

Witherspoon checked the other body 'By the way, what is a Nazi?'

'Are you having me on? Those fucks we just buried are all Nazi scum. They want to take over the bloody world under a bloody madman.'

'Who's that?' Witherspoon looked puzzled as Macbeth and Simms arrived. Macbeth looked at the bodies and the muskets. 'What the hell is this, Bastille day? Why are they firing at us for, we are supposed to be on the same side.'

'Maybe they just clocked the Jerry and opened up' said Simms.

Macbeth looked flustered and strutted about thinking what to do next. Evans suggested they bury the two French soldiers before they get to ripe and finish up at the cottage. Macbeth agreed and assigned Witherspoon and Simms to the French graves and Evans and the young gunner to finish back filling the Garman graves. Evans told Witherspoon he would bring the spades over as soon as they had finished.

As Macbeth left to go back to the cottage, Witherspoon and Simms picked out a shady spot under a tree to rest. Each took a drink from Witherspoon's replenished water bottle and made themselves as comfortable as they could while they waited for the spades to show up.

Simms removed his boots and massaged his sore feet. Witherspoon gave him what he called medicinal oil from his pack. Simms poured the scented oil on his feet and rubbed it in to his relief.

'Thanks, that is wonderful oil.' Simms handed the small bottle back to Witherspoon and spread his reeking socks out to dry. 'Don't suppose you seen that little monkey hereabouts Simmo? Lovely little chap, just ran off somewhere.'

'Can't say I have. He might turn up when he gets hungry.'

'I hope so.' Witherspoon replied. He pointed at the French soldiers. 'Might queer these goings on Simmo, might queer indeed. These chaps firing on us like that.'

'These are turbulent times Witherspoon, and can you wonder when a man loses his mind,' said Simms, chewing on a blade of grass. 'I've been seen some strange things that I have. I saw a chap run at a machine gun post stark naked he was, just his boots, rifle and bayonet. Wedding tackle flapping in the wind. Funny thing was, the Bosch stopped firing. I think they were just taken aback like.'

'What happened to the poor bugger?' 'Well, he got within twenty yards, shouting and hollerin, when they opened up and shredded the chap.'

'That's terrible. Did he get a medal,?' asked Simms.

'No, he got fuck all, like the rest of us. I seen some awful things. I was in Ypres when the first gas attack came over. Men coughing their lungs out. Awful goings on, them there Bosh don't fight fair you see,' said Witherspoon taking another swallow from his water bottle.

'Sounds pretty grim, don't know where that is but I'm glad I wasn't there.'

'Don't like to talk ill of the dead, but is your corporal the full ticket like?'

Simms laughed and stood up as the young gunner turned up with the spades. The three soldiers dug into the hard clay soil and buried both bodies in the same hole.

Witherspoon gathered up their bits and pieces, muskets and headgear and dropped them into the grave. They stood awkwardly beside the opening as Witherspoon recited the lord's prayer. They took turns to backfill the grave owing to the heat while Simms fashioned two pieces of fallen branch together to make a cross. He knocked it down with the butt of his Enfield before the soldiers made their way back to the cottage.

Macbeth was busy filling the German soldiers' water bottles from the pump as they entered the kitchen.

'Good, you're back. I want to get going as quick as we can, before anyone else takes a pot at us.' He handed each man a full water bottle before gathering the troop outside. 'Have you found the radio corp,' asked Simms.

'Boyce found it in the garden smashed up, you can have a look at it if you want.' Macbeth gestured towards the vegetable garden. Simms examined what was left of the radio. All the valves smashed, and the wiring pulled apart. Although he was disappointed to see the set damaged in this way, he was glad that at least he didn't have to carry it anymore.

Boyce had made up a new uniform from spare sheets he had found in a cupboard. After wrapping his groin area, he flung the extra material over his shoulder in the form of a Toga. He also came across some net curtains, which he cut up and placed over his helmet and tied loosely around his neck to keep the flies off. Macbeth had given up trying to keep the men's uniforms in some sort of army order.

With a wave of his hand, he led his band of brothers forward down the track, back into the woods. The trees at least gave some shade from the sun and the dappled light bounced off their helmets. 'Are we heading south corp?' asked Evans. 'Yes, at lest I think we are. This track must lead

somewhere. It looks well used if you look at the ruts.' At that moment, there came a deep roaring sound in the distance. The mob stood still and listened intently, looking around and at each other. The roar came again and echoed through the dark crevices between the trees and faded away.

'What the fuck was that?' said Boyce. He checked the safety on his Thompson.

Macbeth told the others what he had seen back at the bomb site regarding the empty circus wagons. 'You mean we have been walking around with bloody lions hunting us.' said Evans. 'And there might be a few Tigers as well. They've probably gone off to hunt some deer or something,' added Macbeth.

'That's great that is, now we have to dodge the bloody jerries and hungry Lions' as well,' piped Boyce. 'They are just circus animals, trained to jump through hoops, and the like,' Macbeth was trying to calm the men. 'Sounds like the British Army corp' said Simms.

'Have you got a Whip and a kitchen chair handy. Anyway, if the bugger shows up, it will have to feast on the slowest runner,' said Evans, looking at Boyce.

'Alright, just calm down now. I think you are forgetting that we are heavily armed. If they show up, we can just pot the buggers.' Macbeth moved off down the track and the others followed, keeping an extra eye on the darker parts of the wood.

The gaggle moved on down the track, keeping ears tuned and eyes peeled.

The clammy heat became oppressive, and the trees and the ferns started to give way to more lighter patches.

Macbeth stopped more frequently and the water bottles became lighter. Unfamiliar sounds came echoing out from the dense tree line as the soldiers made their way along the track.

Chapter 6

The Procession slogged along nonchalantly. Gaps started to manifest as the men bunched up to converse. Witherspoon joined up with the young gunner.

'How are you feeling now, lad?'

'Not too bad thanks, I would like to thank you for helping me.'

'Think nothin of of it you. We have to look out for each other, I be a reckoning.' replied the big man, smiling.

The boy looked down at the ground, trying to concentrate his mind. 'Still can't remember anything. Do you think I will ever get my memory back?'

'Of course you will lad, tis just a temporary malady you have, that's all. Once you have time to heal and we sort out the Hun, we can all go home.'

The Young gunner removed his helmet and mopped his brow. 'I get flashbacks of things, but I don't know if they are real or imagined. Can't remember even getting here.'

'Don't try to force it you. Everything will come back in its own good time. You concentrate on getting better. We should stop for tea soon and I might just 'ave a little surprise for you in my pack.' The big man winked and put his index finger to his lips.

The trees started to grow apart, allowing more of the cobalt blue sky to amaze them. It opened up upon a small clearing. A dilapidated wooden building was slowly decaying and rotting off to one side. Some rusted cutting tools lay scattered about, an old axe head and saw. The shingled roof half collapsed. The mist had retreated and evaporated as quickly as it had appeared. Boyce, whose net curtains opened up and tied around his helmet, examined the building and wandered around it, appearing on the far side with an old wooden wheelbarrow. He placed it in a shaded spot and positioned his pack towards the handle end, before clambering in, his bare, bony legs dangling over the side, his boots acting like pendulums. Wrapping his toga around his shoulders, he made himself as comfortable as he could before closing his eyes to knap.

Macbeth viewed Boyce settling himself with indifference. He was just as tired and fed up as the rest, but he was in charge. It was down to him to lift the spirits of the men. So he called for tea.

Simms made ready for a brew. He decided to make a small fire to save on paraffin. The fire, made from the roof shingles, soon erupted, a kettle hung precariously over the flame. The Enamel cups appeared, given a quick rinse and wipe before being lined up along a log. The men found shady spots to rest. Witherspoon sat down next to the young gunner and, true to his word, produced a metal flask and unscrewed the top. Checking they were not being observed, he handed over the flask. The unmistakable aroma of brandy wafted from the vial as the boy lifted the spout to his lips. 'There you go now lad, you get that down you. Purely medicinal now you understand, don't let on to the others about it, will you? I 'ave been a saving it for emergencies like.'

The youth took a swallow of the golden liquid and, as it burned its way down his chest, he coughed and choked on its intensity. He felt a sudden rush of euphoria as the spirit flowed through his veins and pumped out through his heart. A feeling of calm took over him as a small thrush perched on his boot, a wriggling caterpillar clamped in its beak.

Witherspoon did his best to fend off the flies and midges as they buzzed around. A curious hollow sound entered the arena in fits and starts. Over the normal chatter of birds and insects came the ominous snore of Boyce, fast asleep in the barrow. Macbeth looked over at the sleeping Boyce, mouth wide open, and it seems so repellent even the flies and midges kept their distance. His nose vibrated with each inhale. A sight only a mother could love. The tea was mashed and poured out, the dark brown liquid steamed in the mugs. The hot drink, even without milk, was refreshing. After a reasonable time had elapsed, Macbeth roused himself and stretched. The other men slowly got themselves ready and Boyce was awoken abruptly as Macbeth tipped him out of the wheelbarrow.

Boyce landed badly, skinning both knees and pulling the toga up between his legs squashed his testicles. He rolled around on the ground trying to slacken the toga, unable to cry out.

Red faced, he grunted and groaned. Looking around for sympathy he found none, the pulsating pain had returned to his groin. He cursed the corporal under his breath and moved around the back of the shack to relieve himself. The remains of a big, black crow lay stiff on the ground. Boyce carefully parted his toga, aimed his purple and yellow penis by manipulating his hips and urinated all over the dead bird, forming a mini amber lake around it.

With the kettle and mugs stowed, packs, rifles and other equipment readied. Macbeth, leading the way, marched off at a brisk pace after their rest and soon covered the next mile. Evans, being over a foot taller that Macbeth, soon outpaced the little corporal and took point, striding off down the road. Macbeth just let him go, he was just going to march at his normal walking pace, after all he thought, we are not in a race. As the little corporal mused on these thoughts, he observed Evans moving off the road into the trees ahead. Macbeth hurried forward, monitoring the spot where Evans had entered the wood.

Just as Macbeth was approaching the area, Evans reappeared. 'Better come and have a look at this corp.'

Macbeth followed him through the ferns, crunching on the brown fallen leaves until he stopped and looked up. Perched between two thick branches was a man hanging from a parachute harness. He seemed lifeless, swinging gently in the small breeze drifting among the trees. The white silk canopy draped over the branches above him gave him a sort of theatrical aura.

As the corporal pondered on this new situation, the other soldiers arrived and soon they were all gathered, looking up at the innocuous parachutist swaying above them. Macbeth looked over at Simms. 'Just the man I wanted, Simmo. Shimmy up there and cut that bloke down.' ordered Macbeth.

Simms looked up at yet another tree. He was about to make a complaint, but thought better of it. He knew it would get him nowhere, and the chap was only ten feet off the ground. Simms reluctantly unloaded his pack and rifle. Evans stood at the base of the tree to give him a hand up. He climbed the bottom section quite easily and established a good foothold hauling himself up to the next level. He clambered on up and sat astride a large branch. Inching himself along, he was able to clamber over

124

another higher limb and get himself above the hanging man.

Simms assessed the situation before pulling out his penknife blade, 'If I cut these cords, he's going to drop like a stone.' Simms shouted down.

'It won't matter if he's dead, will it? See if you can get to him and check his vitals.' Macbeth shouted back.

Simms looked down to see if there was a way to reach the man. He slid down the branch and leaned over to grab another one lower down. Easing himself over, he grabbed the parachutist's arm and pulled the man to him.

'He's still alive corp. We need to lower him down. I may need some help up here,' said Simms as he readjusted his position.

Without being ordered, Evans went to help Simms get the parachutist down. They cut the last of the supporting cords and lowered him into Witherspoon's arms. The big man laid him down gently and unbuckled his harness. Evans pulled the snagged canopy out and it dropped to the leaf covered ground. Boyce circled around the group, eyeing the copious amount of silk material that had literally fallen from the sky.

Witherspoon dowsed his forehead with water. The airman stirred and opened his eyes. Witherspoon gave him a drink from the water bottle.

'He's a Yank. Look at his uniform. Must have been shot down nearby.' Evans said.

Macbeth kneeled down next to the airman.

'Surly not Evans, shot down nearby. I wonder how he ended up here then.' Macbeth scoffed and looked the airman over. Witherspoon unzipped his flying suit. Emblazoned across the airman's chest was the name SHERMAN. 'Apparently, his name is Sherman. Definitely a yanky doodle.' said Witherspoon.

The American opened his eyes and looked around. He rubbed his sore head. 'Where the hell am I?' he croaked.

'You be with friends now matey, we'll look after you OK?' replied Witherspoon, handing him his water bottle. The Airman drank in large gulps, and spat some of the water back out.

'Christ, have you been pissing in this canteen, buddy?' He handed back the water bottle.

Witherspoon took back his water bottle, somewhat offended by the airman's attitude. 'I don't piss in water bottles. This is all the water we could find out here.'

The American looked up for the first time at Witherspoon's face. 'Sorry bud, I didn't mean any offence. I'm still not sure how I got here. Have you found anyone else from my plane?' 'No, you are the only one. But we will keep our eyes open for any more. Can you tell me your name and do you know where we are?' asked Macbeth.

'It's Sherman. William Sherman, people call me Bill.'

Witherspoon looked at Sherman's bloody scalp. 'You got a nasty bang on the bonce there matey, I'll have to dress that.

Macbeth was eager to question the airman.

'Can you tell us what's the latest news, we have been out of touch for some time?' asked Macbeth earnestly.

Sherman had the same sort of look on his face that the boy gunner had, one of confused bewilderment. He felt the wound on his head. A lump had grown the size of a golf ball.

Eventually he said, 'Dammed if I can remember much at all. I know where I come from, where I was born, but nothing recent.

That's really strange.'

While the others had been occupied, Boyce had cut the parachute up. He folded up the sections of the silk he intended to keep and placed them inside his kit bag next to his collectables. He then nonchalantly circled back towards the track.

Macbeth nodded to Evans to speak in private. Macbeth removed his helmet and scratched his sweat coated bandana. He looked over at Evans for advice. Evans looked over at the

American airman. 'He's in no condition to walk. We'll have to make up a litter or something and carry him.'

'I've got a better idea,' said Macbeth, a wry smile on his face. 'Boyce!'

Boyce looked up when the corporal shouted his name. He thought he was in for a bollocking for stealing the parachute. He moved over to where Macbeth was standing with Evans.

'Boyce, I won't you to go back to that old woodshed and bring back the wheelbarrow. We can use that to transport the yank airman.' ordered Macbeth.

Boyce cursed his luck and the corporal under his breath. Macbeth gave him a cutting look. He sloped off back down the track, mumbling to himself. Before heading off, he hid his pack and the Thompson among the ferns, not wanting to carry any unnecessary weight.

The heat was getting to him, so he made a copy of Witherspoon's hanki hat from the parachute silk. After donning this and making some adjustments to the knots, he was satisfied. As Boyce waddled up the track, he thought up ways to get back at Macbeth. Like, as the yank had suggested, urinating in his water bottle or collecting the fleas off some dead animal and slipping them in his trousers when he dozed.

Presently he came to an intersection which he could not remember passing before. He stood at the crossroads, looking in all four directions and wondering why he hadn't noticed this on the way past. Boyce adjusted his toga and waddled on. He had only covered about 100 yards when a strange noise came echoing through the trees. Sound in the forest bounced off trees and could travel some distance from the source. He thought about the circus animals running abroad. Pricking up his ears, he stood still and heard the winning and snorting of a horse. He caught a movement through the trees and moved himself off the track and into the ferns, just keeping his head above the tops of the swaying leaves.

The movement he saw now hove into view. A man came riding up the intersecting trackway. A man on horseback. He was dressed as a Roman Centurion, a brightly plumed helmet upon his head. As he reached the intersection, he stopped and looked around, deciding which track he should follow. The Roman officer seemed to look straight at him. Boyce slowly cowed down and hoped he hadn't been spotted. What seemed like an age Boyce heard the rider move off, keeping to the original track from whence he came.

Boyce emerged from the ferns and watched as the horseman trotted off around a bend and disappeared among the trees. He thought the morphine was still active in his system, giving him flashbacks and hallucinations. Boyce decided not the tell the others as they would only mock him and say he was making it up. After adjusting his groin area, he shuffled off to pursue his quest to retrieve the wheelbarrow.

Half walking and half waddling another half a mile, Boyce found the old dilapidated shed and checked the wheelbarrow. Turning it upside down, he spun the wheel, which squeaked and stopped after a few turns. Ferreting among the contents of the shed, Boyce found a near-empty can of grease. He managed to scrape out a small quantity of the green paste and applied the sticky substance to the axle, freeing up the rotation of the wooden wheel.

The handles were baking hot and cracked, so Boyce looked around for something he could use to wrap them.

He then noticed the old crow that he had urinated on had disappeared, replaced in the centre of his dried up puddle by the paw print of an enormous cat. Boyce felt a strange shiver cascade down his backbone. He looked around the clearing to see if he was being watched. The only movement were kits chasing each other and leaping from branch to branch.

Sprinkling some water over his hanki hat, he moved nervously off, back down the track. With the extra weight of the wheelbarrow, Boyce had developed a peculiar gait, which caused the barrow to oscillate. Every few hundred yards, Boyce would stop and listen. Then, to his dismay, came the unmistakable low growl of an enormous cat some distance away. He doubled his efforts, pushing the heavy barrow before him at a semi-run swagger, with the thought that the animal had got his scent and was looking for the tender morsel of his bum cheek.

Simms felt sorry for the American and came over to offer him a cup of tea. Sherman said he would prefer coffee if he had it. 'Sorry, we only have tea and no milk. You will be right as rain when you've had a cuppa mate.'

Simms pumped the paraffin vessel and put the kettle on, using up his last supply of water. While he waited for the kettle to boil, he asked the airman where he was from.

'I'm from Boston, Massachusetts. I've never been out of the states before coming here, to Europe that is, wherever this is.' Sherman stood up and held onto a tree branch to steady himself.

'That's a good question.' Simms looked around to see if he was being overheard. 'We don't have a clue, mate. I was hoping you, being an airman and all, would have seen something before bailing out.'

Sherman looked around the forest at the trees, the small amount of sky above. 'Bailing out of what? I don't remember anything after leaving the States. Sorry bud, I don't remember a thing.'

'That makes two of you. That boy over there can't even remember his name.' Simms nodded towards the young gunner.

Boyce stopped to rest. He sat down in among the ferns and then laid back, allowing his aching muscles to relax. Pulling some dried leaves over his legs like a brown blanket he laid back and stared up at two turtle pigeons. The male trying to approach the female from behind and the female turning around to thwart the males advances.

He then suddenly realised that he had nothing to protect himself with, having left his Thompson back with the others. With this thought galloping through his brain, he cursed and he rose up like Lazarus from the ferns and hurried on his way.

After some time, he came to the spot where he had hid from the Roman horseman. He recognised the trampled ferns. He pushed the barrow down the milled track another hundred yards and found no sign of the intersection. Nothing was there. He looked back up the way he had come and was certain this was where the

Roman horseman had passed. Yet there was no intersection. Again, he put it down to the morphine. Maybe he imagined the big cat as well, he thought. He strutted on, feeling a little relieved that maybe the animal was, after all, just a figment of his imagination. Feeling a little better, he slowed his pace until the faint rumble of an enormous cat echoed around him again. He waddled on as fast as he could.

'Where the hell is that bloody cockney sparrow got to? I'll bet the lazy fucker is sleeping somewhere, scaring the local wildlife.' said Macbeth, looking back up the road. Boyce was nowhere to be seen.

Simms looked over Macbeth's shoulder up the rutted trackway. 'He'll be alright, he's as tough as old nails that one'

'He's the colour of old nails more like.' Macbeth chuckled at his own joke, throwing away the dregs of his tea.

Witherspoon dressed the airman's wound and made up a bandage to wrap around his head like a turban. He gave him a small draught of brandy, for medicinal reasons. He asked Sherman not to say anything to the others about the spirit.

Boyce could be heard from some distance away, the wheelbarrow rumbling down the track. Pushing the barrow to one side, he collapsed among the ferns, red of face and breathing heavy.

Simms went to check on him. 'You alright Boyce?'

Boyce rolled over and sat up, rubbing his red, tear-stained face with his toga. 'I was nearly bloody eaten back there by a bleedin' Lion or somat. The fucker followed me back here.' He gasped. 'The cunt has my scent and wants to bite my arse.'

Macbeth, hearing the rant, chuckled to himself. 'I doubt it. Even a bloody Lion has better taste than that. The way you stink Boyce, any self respecting Lion would leave your reeking carcass to the hyenas.'

'What hyenas? I didn't know about any fucking hyenas.' bellowed Boyce.

'There are a few around Boycey, but they are scavengers. They are after the dead or nearly dead. Mind you, the way you stink, they would probably think you were a corpse anyway.' replied Macbeth.

The corporal's remarks did not reassure Boyce and turning a peculiar shade of white mixed with the red and blue of his groin, torso and legs, he took on the appearance of a human chameleon. He retrieved his Thompson, vowing it would never leave his side again.

After some cajoling, Sherman reluctantly sat in the wheelbarrow. He shared the cart with rifles, packs and other equipment. Once settled, the troop moved off, following the way that Macbeth thought was south. The corporal took the lead. The young gunner stepped forward to take the first turn, pushing the now very heavy wheelbarrow. He felt physically better now and wanted to help as much as he could. Boyce kept to the middle of the formation, ears pricked for any strange sounds emanating from the deep, dense, lion infested wood.

They made good time covering the next few miles. The terrain started to drop, and the soldiers descended into a valley. The little corporal knew that at the bottom they would probably find some form of water course. A chance to refill their water bottles would give the men a boost, he knew, especially now, without the radio. They were completely cut off from the world. He also knew the track must lead somewhere, as Evans had said, and he must keep the men's spirits up. He looked back at the motley crew following up behind and smiled.

'Did you see that, Evans? I think napoleon is going off his rocker.' said Simms.

'Never mind about the corp. He's got a lot on his plate at the moment.' replied Evans.

Simms took his turn with the wheelbarrow and found the going hard on his arms and legs. The American dosed in the heat and the gentle swaying of the barrow. They sauntered on at an easy pace. The birds tweeted and chirped their merry songs to help the soldiers on their way.

Witherspoon never heard the shot. He just felt a thump in his chest. Blood started to ooze from the wound spreading around his waistband.

Chapter 7.

The report of the rifle shot echoed through the avenue. There was a moment of disbelief as the troop stopped and, as if in slow motion, the thwack of the bullet impacted on Witherspoon's chest, sending the big man stumbling back. All the men dived into the ferns. Simms tipped the wheelbarrow over and dragged the struggling airman into the relative safety among the foliage. Witherspoon stood stock still on the track, looking down at the blood now issuing across his vest. Evans dashed out to help Witherspoon but was forced back as another shot rang out, the bullet catching Evan' s helmet rim. He dived back into the trees and shouted to Witherspoon to get off the track.

The big man just stood still and felt the wound with the tips of his fingers. He moved forward down the track mumbling to himself that he was alright and he was going home. All the men were shouting at him to take cover, but it was in vain. Witherspoon just ignored them, stumbling on in full view of their assailant.

Evans knew the shooter was waiting for someone to go to the wounded man's aid, to expose themselves to his next bullet.

Suddenly, Boyce sprung up out the ferns like a man possessed, and let loose with the Thompson, giving the tree line the entire magazine in one burst. He sprayed the trees and foliage where he thought the last shot had come from. As the Tommy gun spat and bucked out its rounds, Boyce screamed at the shooter.

Evans now took the chance to dart out and pull Witherspoon back among the trees. He laid him down on the ground and peeled back his blouse, exposing the blood stained vest beneath. Evans fished out a spare vest from his pack and applied it to the wound. He applied pressure to stem the blood loss. Witherspoon was turning white, a grey green hue formed under his eyes and his breathing became erratic and heavy.

There were shouts from the others that Boyce had evidently killed the sniper with his burst. 'How' s Witherspoon, Evans?' asked the young gunner as he ran to help.

'Not good'

The boy crawled over to Witherspoon to see if he could help.

Tears were forming as he surveyed his friend's blood stained chest. 'Hold this over the wound, keep the pressure on it. Evans sat Witherspoon against a tree to make him more comfortable. He opened his water bottle and held it to Witherspoon's chapped lips, tipping the liquid carefully into his mouth.

'You'll be ok mate, we'll have you sorted and right as rain,' croaked the young gunner, trying hard to keep his voice normal.

The big man just sat staring ahead. Evans cleaned the wound by pouring water over the area and applying a shell dressing and wrapping a bandage tightly around his chest. 'I'm ok, I'm alright, just give me a few minutes to rest,' gasped Witherspoon. 'I'm going home now, I going home to see my good wife. I think I'd done my bit now for King and Country.' The boy offered his water bottle to Witherspoon. He put the spout to his mouth and tipped the bottle forwards to moisten his blueing lips. The water ran down the side of his cheek.

Evans looked for any morphine in Witherspoon's pack. He fished out an ampoule and, breaking off the end, injected the contents into his arm.

Witherspoon seemed to respond immediately as he stood up and walked out through the ferns and stumbled down the road. Evans and the boy tried to stop him, but he seemed to have the strength of ten men and bayed them to leave him be. 'I'm going home now.' Witherspoon said to no one in particular. 'I want to see my Mable and the kids.' He stared off down the track and raised his arm to point the way home. The young gunner ran after him. 'Please rest now mate, we can patch you up and then when you get better you can go home and see your missus.' pleaded the boy, tears rolling down his face.

Witherspoon just stared down the track as Boyce and Simms dragged a body out of the foliage onto the track.

He walked on by mumbling to himself, repeating over and over that he was alright and not to fuss. He was going home.

The boy followed, pleading with him.

The gentle giant stopped and stood still, staggered to his left before collapsing into the ditch. He was dead before he hit the ground. Evans turned his body over and closed

Witherspoon's eyes.

The men came up one by one to gaze upon their fallen comrade. Simms walked off to get the wheelbarrow. After carefully wrapping his body in a groundsheet, they wheeled it back to a shaded area under the trees. Evans marked out the grave and began digging.

Macbeth came over to look at the German sniper. He removed his SS helmet to reveal a boy of around sixteen years old. His blue eyes clouding over. Blond, wet hair stuck to his forehead. 'He's just a bloody kid. Not even shaving yet.' mumbled Macbeth.

'Still did for Witherspoon, though.' said Simms. Macbeth tasked Boyce with disposing of the sniper's body. After checking his pockets for anything of value. All Boyce found was a dogeared photograph of his family, the dead boy smiling, dressed in a scout uniform. His proud mother and father standing behind in happier days. Boyce ripped it in half and tossed it over the dead boy's face. He scraped away at the topsoil in a ditch on the side of the track and dug down just enough to cover the corpse. After dragging the already decomposing body into the shallow grave, Boyce threw in the sniper's rifle and covered him over. Finishing the job with some ferns and dried leaf droppings.

The young gunner helped Evans dig the grave. In the short time he had known Witherspoon, he had become very fond of the big man. They took it in turns to dig as the heat sapped their strength. When the grave was deep enough, the soldiers carried their comrade over and placed him gently in the cool earth. Evans backfilled the soil over his dead friend, a lump forming in his throat. He smoothed over and humped the red soil into a neat pile and stood back to survey his work.

Macbeth removed his helmet and sweat soaked bandana before clearing his throat. He looked at each soldier before saying, 'I am not a religious man and I don't think Witherspoon was either. I have not known him long, but in the short time that I have known him, I found him to be a kind and gentle soul. He was big in stature and full of humility. He, like most men in this shitty war, has been taken before their time.' Macbeth's voice quivered. 'I will never forget the man lying here before us.' He then fell silent and stood one pace back.

As no one else moved forward, Sherman thought he would say a few words. 'I know that I have just come among you men, but Witherspoon was the one who helped me. He nursed me the best he could and would, I suspect, help anyone in distress.' Sherman stood to attention and saluted. The others looked at each other and stood to attention and saluted. Evans held up Witherspoon's back pack. 'There are some letters in here to his wife that he didn't have time to send.' The young gunner stepped forward and asked if he may have them and he would see that the letters were sent. All nodded in agreement without saying a word.

'I didn't know that Witherspoon was married. He never mentioned a wife to me.' said Simms, walking away from the grave with Evans. 'He said nothing to me about that side of his life, or that he had kids as well.' Simms looked at Evans.

'Christ, I never thought about that. Did you read any of his letters?'

'No, I didn't. They were personal to his wife.' snapped Evans.

Alright, I was only asking, just curious, that's all.' Macbeth picked up Witherspoon's rifle and fixed the bayonet. He thrust it into the ground at the head of the grave and placed

Witherspoon's helmet across the butt end. He looked around to make sure no one was looking at him before making the cross with his hand over the grave. Under his breath he said, 'May your God be with you, old chap, and bless you for all your help.' He had to wipe something from his eye with his filthy bandana as he gathered the troop together.

The corporal told Boyce to keep the wheelbarrow and that he was personably responsible for it. Sherman had recovered enough to walk with the others, so they heaped the wheelbarrow with rifles and packs. Boyce cursed Macbeth under his breath.

There came a slight breeze as the gaggle started off, giving the men a lift in their demeanour. The catastrophic heat had sapped physical and mental strength from each man. Tensions were mounting among the group and Macbeth was concerned that they would rebel against him and go off on their own. Worse still was not knowing where they were or what was going on outside the endless forest. Moral was at rock bottom. Macbeth stopped to have a drink from his water bottle, which felt concerningly light.

Evans came up behind him and said he would take point and scout the area in front. Macbeth just nodded.

The bedraggled troop came up the track, heads bowed and deep in their own thoughts. No one was talking. Macbeth called for a tenminute rest and each man found a shady spot to rest in

Sherman sat down next to Simms and offered him a cigarette. 'Thanks, I've almost run out.' 'I'll have a fag, Yank,' said Boyce, stepping over to get it.

Sherman fished out another Lucky Strike from an old tobacco tin and handed it to Boyce.

'Thanks yank, you are not so bad after all, you may even come in useful.' Boyce said as he turned and sat back down, caressing the cigarette.

Sherman looked at Boyce's attire and, turning to Simms, said, 'I take it that's not standard uniform?'

'Don't ask, I won't bore you with all that.' Simms lit up and puffed the luxurious blue smoke out. 'Well, that is good.

Thanks for that.'

'You're welcome. Tell the truth, I have never been out of my home state of Massachusetts before, let alone the US.

Macbeth barked a lethargic order to resume their trek. The soldiers gathered together and loped off down the road. Boyce pleaded with Simms to take over the wheelbarrow, as he was experiencing some acute pain in the bottom of his stomach. Simms felt sorry for Boyce, who was looking and smelling worse than ever. He reminded him of something he had seen in a Boris Karloff film. Simms only agreed if Boyce walked some yards behind the troop, acting as rear guard. Boyce was hesitant owing to the exposure of a Lion attack. He relented as Simms was about to walk off without the wheelbarrow. Boyce cradled his Thompson like a comfort blanket. If the lion makes an appearance, thought Boyce, little Tommy would sort him out. He patted the wooden stock affectionately.

The little corporal re-tied his bandanna and adjusted his helmet. He was about to move off when Evans appeared around a bend and came hurrying towards them, waving his hand. Macbeth went to meet him.

'Bloody Jerry tank up ahead, just sitting there in the middle of the road. Couldn't see if the crew were in there or not.' Macbeth called the men to gather around.

'What do you reckon then, Evans? Asked the corporal.

Evans took a drink from his water bottle and said that the tank was not moving and they should close in from two sides. Macbeth looked at Evans closely as he suspected the Welshman was taking the mick. Evans managed to keep a straight face.

'That sounds like a pincer movement corp.' Boyce said from the back. Simms laughed as

Macbeth's face turned even redder. 'Alright, alright, very bloody funny, I'm sure. We will all proceed forward and have a gander together, gentlemen.' Macbeth moved off, mumbling to himself. The others followed on with Boyce, constantly looking over his shoulder, bring up the rear. Apart from the clump of hobnailed boots, a new sound had joined the men, a squeaky wheelbarrow wheel. The grease had worn off and friction had made the barrow harder to push.

Within a few hundred yards, as Macbeth rounded a bend, the Black menacing form of a Panzer tank hove into view. As Evans has said, it was just sitting there in the middle of the track. The tank pointed away from him. The barrel of its gun obscured by the turret.

 Macbeth moved the men off into the cover of the ferns and gathered them together. 'I going forward with Evans to take a better look at this bugger. You lot stay here and don't make any noise or brew up' Macbeth looked at Simms and the grinning Boyce.

 Macbeth and Evans removed their kit and helmets and moved off through the trees, keeping to the left side of the track, out of sight of any possible occupants inside the tank. Sherman sat down next to Simms and removed his boots. 'My feet are getting blistered with all this walking.' 'You don't do much marching then, Sherman?' asked Simms.

 'I'm a flyboy, we ride the clouds, hell we even get taken out to our aircraft in a jeep.' 'Wasn't there a General called William Sherman? Sherman looked at Simms in surprise. 'I bow to your knowledge. My full name is William Tecumseh Sherman. My dad was an amateur historian. He specialized in the civil war.' Sherman opened his tin and handed Simms a Lucky Strike. Simms took the cigarette. 'Thanks. Where did Tecumseh come from?

 'He was apparently a Shawnee chief. So I got stuck with his name.' Sherman flicked open his zippo and lit both cigarettes.

 Simms sucked in the blue smoke, 'Didn't he burn down Atlanta?'

'He did, they love him down there in the south.' Sherman rubbed at his feet with a doc leaf.

Macbeth and Evans made their way through the trees and undergrowth, keeping to the left side of the road. Nearing the static Panzer, they circled around a large fallen Oak. Macbeth found a foothold in the rough bark and hosted himself up to observe the tank at close quarters. Evans joined him and the two men listened intently for any noise or movement. They heard nothing apart from the usual sounds of the forest. The crows cawing and small animals scuttling around in the undergrowth.

The metal tank looked impotent sitting in the middle of the track like some dead carnivore.

The little corporal mopped his forehead and squeezed out his bandanna. He turned to Evans and whispered, 'I'm going in. You stay here and cover me. If any bugger comes out of that tin can, pot the fucker.' He retied his spotted head covering and slid down the trunk of the Oak cursing as he fell off and caught a bent branch between his legs. His eyes watered as his lower stomach went into a schism of unparalleled pain. Paralyzed, he lay among the ferns trying to breathe.

'You alright corp?' Evans said, looking down at Macbeth lying motionless, staring at the sky. His hands cupped over his genitalia. Macbeth moaned as his lungs filled with oxygen and he rolled over, flattening the ferns and murmuring, 'God all fucking mighty.' After a few minutes, he crawled around on his knees and then stood up, using the tree trunk to support himself.

Evans repeated his question, 'You alright corp, do you want me to go?'

Macbeth gathered himself and replied in a hoarse voice, 'I'm OK, just landed funny, that's all, bit winded.' He made his unsteady way around the fallen trunk and crouched down as he broke cover. He hobbled over to the Panzer and braced himself against the hull.

Thick dried mud covered the metal and rubber tracks. Shell and small arms damage were evident on the hull and turret. The painted white and black cross faded and discoloured. Macbeth slipped his hand down the front of his trousers and carefully massaged his tender scrotum sack. He felt some relief as he manipulated his delicate testicles within the sack. He looked up to see Evans staring down at him.

The corporal turned around and withdrew his hand. He fished out a mills bomb and held it up for Evans to see. The corporal made his way to the front and clambered up, using the centre boss of the tank wheel as a foothold. He climbed onto the hull and sat near the open hatch on the turret.

Still hearing nothing from inside the tank, he would not take any chances. He pulled the pin on the Mills and was about to drop it through the hatch.

Evans waved his arms in the air, trying to attract Macbeth's attention, but the corporal was too intent on carrying out his task to look up. As Macbeth was about to drop the grenade through the hatch, Evans stood up on the tree trunk and shouted, 'Don't throw that fucking grenade in there, you stupid cunt!'

Macbeth froze with a mixture of anger and humiliation. He was being ordered about by a mere squaddie. He now, red faced, looked up at Evans.

Evans looked down at the ginger NCO and said, 'Have you noticed that pool of diesel fuel under the engine cowling? And there might be a working radio in there.'

Corporal Macbeth ingested the information and knew Evans was right. But his authority was being undermined again. Evans jumped down from the tree trunk and signalled for the others to come up.

'Evans, help me find the pin for this bloody thing, will you?' Macbeth said sternly, dismounting the tank. The two men circled around each other, poking through the undergrowth. As the other men arrived, Macbeth gave the grenade to Simms with the explicit instruction not to let it go.

Evans stopped looking for the pin and decided his time was better spent examining the interior of the tank.

Climbing up to the turret, he looked down inside the white painted hull. He was careful to check for any booby traps that the departing crew may have left. Seeing nothing, he lowered himself down. The interior felt claustrophobic.

Evans opened the side hatches to let more air and light in. It smelled of diesel fumes, body odour and cordite. Shells lined the wall, held in place with restraints.

148

Different coloured bands decorated the nose end of each projectile. An empty void near the driver's seat showed that the radio had gone. What happened to the crew? Evans pondered the question as he looked for more clues. Personal photos of wives and girlfriends still adorned the turret. Why did the crew leave these?

Simms was getting agitated and his hand was cramping up. He thought about giving the Mills to Boyce, but thought better of it. He poked his head in the tank and asked Evans if there was anything else he could use. Evans handed him a small piece of wire to secure the mills.

Boyce had been given responsibility of the wheelbarrow again, squeaking his way up he circled the tank and, feeling hot and bothered, took the opportunity to rest. After parking the barrow, he slid under the front end of the Panzer to keep away from the diesel spill. It was cooler under the tank with a slight breeze forced under by the tank's design. Boyce used his swag bag as a pillow and, closing his eyes, fell asleep.

Evans extricated himself from the tank and sat down. Simms walked up and down the track, flexing his hand to relive the cramp. It was then that he noticed there were no tracks leading up to the tank. It must weigh several tons he thought, and left no tracks. He walked around to the front of the tank in case it had reversed itself here. There were no tracks there either. Simms was about to bring this observation to the attention of the corporal when he noticed a large dog some way off running towards them.

'Corporal, there's a big dog coming this way.' shouted Simms.

Macbeth and Evans looked around to see the Alsatian with the side pouches running full speed towards them. The dog had been trained to find food under a tank. The starving canine was hell bent on reaching the Panzer.

Evans grabbed his Enfield and before he could work the bolt, the dog was among them and ran under the tank's hull.

The blast threw the men in all directions. Macbeth lay on the ground, his head spinning and a high-pitched whine throbbing through his ears. Pain made itself known after a few minutes from his buttock area.

Chapter 8.

Smoke billowed out from under the tank as the diesel fuel ignited, vapouring the grass and flaring the brown dry ferns surrounding the tank. The pungent stench permeated the stilted air. Simms had dived for cover as he realised the dog's intent, and Evans had been standing to the side of the tank's hull and was shielded from the blast by the wheels and tracks. Simms looked around to see Macbeth rolling around in obvious distress.

The young gunner was helping Sherman, so was some way off when the dog passed them. Simms and Evans ran over to help Macbeth. Evans could see that the corporal had sustained shrapnel wounds to his buttocks, blood seeping through his karki trousers. Macbeth stiffened as Evans rolled him over. The little corporal winced as Evans unbuttoned his fly and carefully pulled down his trousers, exposing his bloody buttocks.

Macbeth, his ears still ringing, could see Evans saying something but could hear nothing over the terrible ringing that reverberated inside his head. He tried to convey his situation by pointing at his ears and shaking his hands from side to side.

'He can't hear anything,' said Simms. 'Damaged his ear drums I suspect.'

Evans eased Macbeth over on to his front to examine his wounds. 'Go and get

Witherspoon's pack, will you? I think it's in the wheelbarrow.' Blood was still oozing from the several shrapnel wounds. Evans poured the last of his water over the corporal's buttocks to clean the lacerations before applying some antiseptic.

Simms walked around looking for the wheelbarrow, he found it abandoned in front of the Panzer. He retrieved the pack as the young gunner and Sherman arrived. 'What's going on Simms? Is anyone hurt?' Sherman enquired.

'The corporal's got hit in the arse, and his eardrums are fucked,' replied Simms, returning with Witherspoon's pack.

'We need to move him away from this bloody smoke.' coughed Evans. Taking Macbeth under each armpit, the two soldiers dragged the corporal down the track away from the dense black smoke. Macbeth, boots dragging by the toecaps, passed out.

They laid the corporal face down on a shaded grass area.

Evans emptied the contents of Witherspoon's pack and found another morphine syrette, and injected Macbeth. 'That should ease the pain for a while. We will have to remove this shrapnel while he's out.' Evans found a pair of long pincers and some spare bandages among the contents, along with a sharp penknife. He also found a flask of brandy. He used the brandy sparingly to wipe the penknife blade and the pincers.

Evans probed the first laceration with the penknife to see how deep the shrapnel was lodged. He felt resistance only an inch in so changed to the pincers. Feeling his way down and around the object, he fastened onto it and gently pulled it out. After rinsing off the object with brandy. Evans held it up for examination. He looked at Simms as they both realised they were looking at a gold tooth.

After some time, they extracted all the teeth from Macbeth's buttocks. Simms cleaned off the excess blood, crud and dirt, wiped the area with the disinfectant before applying some shell dressings and finished off with bandages. The young gunner looked up and down the track. 'Where's Boyce?'

In all the confusion, the others had completely forgotten about Boyce. They called out his name, and Simms made his way around the other side of the still burning tank.

Simms went back to the abandoned wheelbarrow. He found Boyce's Thompson in the barrow and looked around, shielding his mouth and nose from the dense smoke. He called out for him but received no reply. There was no sign of him.

As he picked up the wheelbarrow and turned to go, he spotted something under the tank's hull. As Simms got closer, he made out a dismembered torso, recognizing immediately the multi coloured groin and remnants of a silk toga. Simms made his way back with the barrow. A new patient was waiting to be conveyed.

Evans now took charge of the troop. The billowing smoke could be seen for miles, and he didn't want to be around if any inquisitive German troops turned up. They gently laid the still unconscious Macbeth in the wheelbarrow, careful to keep him on his side in the foetal position. They made their way quickly past the burning tank, half running, half walking to gain as much distance as possible before slowing. Evans eventually called for a rest. The exhausted men sat or laid down in shaded areas and reached for their water bottles. Most were already drained.

Simms sat next to Sherman, who produced two Lucky Strike cigarettes. Sherman looked at the packet and said, 'not so lucky for your buddy back there,' he lit both with his zippo. Simms blew out the blue smoke. 'He wasn't really a friend of mine. He was his own worse enemy.'

'Why did he smell so bad?' asked Sherman. 'Shouldn't we go back and bury the guy?' 'There's not much left to bury. Anyway, he's going to smell a lot worse now, and we couldn't risk hanging about there. The smoke was acting like a beacon.' Simms adjusted his seating position.

Sherman looked up at the clear blue sky. Not a cloud in sight. 'Will it ever rain in this dammed place? What I would give for a nice cold shower right now. I could stand under it for an hour.

Have you got any water left?'

Simms picked up his water bottle and shook it. 'Afraid not, old chum.' He got up and went to check on Macbeth. He passed the young gunner, fast asleep, perched precariously on a tree root. Oblivious to the insects crawling over his face. Emanating from a tree nearby came the shrill rhythmic call of a chick.

Simms had not heard this continuous squawking sound before. He located the sound coming from a perfectly round hole in the side of a tree. As he gazed up at the hole a bird arrived holding a wriggling insect in it's beck, mainly black and white with a red belly. As the bird clung to the bark outside the hole the chick poked his little head out and grabbed the insect from the parent.

Simms had never seen a woodpecker before.

Life goes on he thought.

The corporal was still out cold. Simms felt his forehead, which was burning up. Dousing the spotted bandana with the dregs of Macbeth's water bottle, he applied it across the top half of his head. He then placed the empty bottle between the slumbering mans legs and looked over at Evans.

The new troop leader was sitting under a tree with the same thought. They had to find water soon.   Macbeth was getting dehydrated and would not last long without fluids. Simms was just about to discuss the situation with Evans when a new sound came to his ear. It was distant. But definitely there, getting slightly louder as he concentrated on what it was and where it was coming from.

Evans now stood up, as could hear the sound as well. It came and went, like a radio frequency bouncing off the clouds. The two soldiers scanned the available heavens above the trees, half expecting more planes. They circled around each other, trying to make out the source.

'What is that? Evans asked.

Sherman now joined the two men, listening. 'That's a vehicle and coming this way, I think.'

Evans and Simms came to the same conclusion and moved Macbeth off the track, hiding him in the ferns. They picked up their Enfield's and checked the safety was off and positioned themselves on one side the road. If a firefight broke out, they didn't want to be hit by friendly crossfire.

The sound of the engine could quite clearly be heard now. The whine of the gearbox and the changing engine note as the revs increased. They still could not determine distance or even direction. Sound in a wooded area played tricks, bouncing around like an echo chamber. 'If this is Jerry, and more than half a dozen, we let the buggers go past. Only fire if I fire first.' Evans said, working the bolt on his rifle.

Sherman picked up the Thompson, not wanting to miss out on any action. The engine revs dropped and started building as the clutch was depressed and a new gear selected. As it turned onto an incline, the laboured engine groaned. The sound was suddenly all around them, bouncing off the trees. Evans kept a lookout one way and Simms the other.

Soon the vehicle came into view, struggling up the shallow incline towards the gathered soldiers. The vehicle was a lorry, painted in a drab blue/grey colour. On the front right-hand mudguard was an RAF roundel, Blue, white with a red centre.

Evans couldn't believe his eyes. He jumped out on to the track, waving the driver down. The lorry jerked to a halt. It stopped some yards away, the engine ticking over, providing the only sound. As far as Evans could see, there was only one occupant. The driver just sat looking at Evans as Simms crept up and poked the barrel of his Enfield through the open window. The driver put both hands in the air and smiled. 'How goes it chaps?' Simms laughed and lowered his rifle.

'Am I glad to see you, mate? Have you got any water with you?'

The driver lowered his arms and climbed out of the lorry cab. 'I got half a dozen jerry cans full in the back.' Replied the driver. 'Where the hell have you come from then?' enquired Sherman as he came up to shake the driver's hand. They all started to talk at once.

Simms clambered in the back of the lorry and opened a Jerry can, pouring out the slightly tainted water into his cupped hands. Evans appeared at the tailgate and Simms passed out the heavy can. Evans filled Macbeth's water bottle and tried to get him to drink. Macbeth stirred. He opened his eyes and looked up at Evans.

'What the fuck happened, Evans?' he mumbled. 'You had a bit of a set to with a dog.' smiled Evans, seeing Macbeth was definitely on the mend.

'Lets have some more water, Evans. I'm parched. My bloody arse feels a bit queer.' Macbeth drank down the diesel tainted water as if it was ginger beer.

'Where did this water come from?' 'You won't believe this.' Evans wheeled the barrow out onto the track and set Macbeth down in front of the RAF lorry.

Macbeth sat up awkwardly and just stared at the vehicle. He then stared at the driver.

'Where the fuck did you come from?'
The lorry driver just smiled and replied, 'Same question I put to your chaps only a few minutes ago, corporal. I seem to have been driving around this forest for hours. I'm lost. As to where I came from, we had orders to abandon our makeshift airfield and head north. I've been

driving ever since.' 'Help me out of this thing, will you, Evans?' Macbeth squirmed from side to side, looking for the very first time vulnerable and helpless. Evans helped the little man stand on his feet. He stood legs apart, stooped over like an old man with haemorrhoids.

'You had a bit of shrapnel in your backside corporal.' said Simms. Macbeth put his hand down his trouser and felt the dressings. He inched forward in his bare feet, wincing as his buttocks clenched and gravel pricked at the souls of his feet.

The driver piped up. 'My name is Parker, leading aircraftsman Parker, known to one and all as Percy. Although my Christian name is Alfred.' He looked around at the assembly and, as no one said anything, he carried on. 'Don't suppose you know the way out of this forest, do you?' again he looked from one blank face to the other. 'Any tarmacked road will do?'

Simms lifted the heavy jerry can and poured water over his head, shaking off the excess like a dog.

'He's as lost as we are. I going to make us all a nice cup of tea.' He turned and marched off down the track, carrying the jerry can to fill his kettle. His hobnail boots clunking on the gravel.

The young gunner woke up with a start, as one determined bug had made its way up his nose and lodged in his throat. Sitting up, he coughed out the bug and wiped his sweated face. Rubbing his stiff neck, he stood up.

There was no sign of the others, just the sweet birdsong to   accompany his
thoughts.   Stretching his aching muscles, he found Witherspoon's private pack and walked off amid the trees, glad to be alone for once. The trees swayed over his head as a gentle breeze had built up and the lush leaves responded with little dances. He walked on until he came out into an open glade. The grass was greener and taller here, with tell-tale pockets of rabbit bumbles to reveal their presence.

A large root stretched out from an old oak, a perfect place to sit. The youth pulled out the bundle of letters from
Witherspoon's pack. Under the dappled light, he looked down at the string bound pile of dogeared letters, wondering whether he should pry.

He decided he needed some Dutch courage and
took a swig of brandy from the flask. The spirit burned its glorious way down his oesophagus as he closed his eyes and felt the intoxicating liquor surge through his veins. Pulling back the string on one edge, he lifted out the top envelope. He found the address on the front had been written in pencil.

My Dearest Mildred.
I baint be pleased to say that things are alright so far. Although my dear, I find myself in a very mixed company at present. Can't say as I got here, I fell asleep thinking of you and the kids in my funk hole and woke to find myself

in a wood. Under a corporal, a nice enough chap but a little 'ooden 'edded like.

How bist e? Hope our kiddies are well and helping you out with all the going on. If that flibbertigibbet Albert is causin' you any bother tell 'im he will answer to me when I get back to Blighty.

Can't stop thinking of you and the kids, my love, and long for the day when we will be together again. I be love you to the farthest reaches of my heart, my dear.

Your true and ever lovin husband Frank.

The boy folded the letter and placed in back in its envelope. He took another swallow of the brandy and lifted his head to allow the spirit to glide down easier. With his eyes again closed, he didn't hear the Lioness approaching him. He just felt the momentary sharp pain as the jaws clamped around his neck, the incisor teeth puncture his windpipe, stopping the scream.

Chapter 9

Simms poured out the dark brown liquid and added some extra boiling water to the pot. The chipped enamel mugs were lined up. By some miracle, the RAF chap had some powdered milk in his cab, which was now added to the mugs. The steaming liquid turned the perfect mid brown colour of nectar.

Simms looked around for the young gunner, checking the spot where he was seen sleeping. There was no sign of him and, after calling several times, he gave up deciding that tea consumption was more important.

Simms managed to convey four mugs of piping hot tea without spilling too much back to the lorry. The group of men settled down with their tea in the shade afforded to them by the side of the lorry canvas canopy.

Macbeth eased himself down on the footplate. Evans having padded the seat with an old hessian blanket from the back of the lorry. He looked around. 'Where's the boy Simmo?'

'I looked for him. He must have slopped off somewhere. He'll turn up.'

Sherman handed out his cigarettes. The blue smoke helped keep the midges and flies off. 'How much fuel do you have, Percy?' asked Evans.

'I reckon on just over half a tank. Should be good for fifty miles or more. Mind you, that's mostly in low gear on these roads, if you can call them that.' No one said anything so he continued, ' I saw smoke on the horizon earlier. Anything to do with you chaps?'

Macbeth sipped his tea, savouring the powdered milk infused liquid. He winked at Evans.

'Had a run in with a Tiger Tank, knocked it out with an anti-tank gun and dispatched the entire crew with a grenade down the hatch.
Bloody thing caught fire, and we had to scarper.'

Parker looked impressed. 'Bloody hell, you chaps have been in the wars. Don't know what I would do if I came up against a Tiger Tank.' 'He's 'avin you on Percy. There was a tank, but not a tiger. One of the small ones, a mark four I think. We found it abandoned a few miles back.' said Simms.

'And you set fire to it? asked Parker. 'A fucking dog blew it up.' said Macbeth, easing his buttocks over to one side. 'Is this still the joke? A dog?' Parker looked puzzled. 'No, that's exactly what happened.' replied Simms, and carried on sipping his tea.

Parker looked even more puzzled. No one was in the mood to explain what had occurred, and no one mentioned Boyce.

Macbeth eased himself off the footplate to lie down. Evans laid out the hessian blanket for the corporal to lie upon. As Macbeth lowered himself down on his stomach, this didn't deter the army of miniature soldier ants from descending and irritating the injured corporal.

Sherman finished his tea and wished it had been coffee. Looking at the tea leaves at the bottom of the mug reminded him of the Gypsy queen, who had read his fortune at Coney Island before embarkation to Europe. She said he was going to go on an adventure after a long sea voyage. He was in uniform and troop ships were leaving every other day. He vaguely remembered the crossing even though it was in a transport plane, not a sea voyage. Parker broke the silence by saying, 'I was a teacher at a boarding school. Taught History, mainly Roman Britain, they were here some time, you know. Four hundred

years, that's a long time.'

'How come you ended up as a driver with your education?' asked Simms.

'I was conscripted and sent to an RAF airfield for training. They trained me to drive a lorry.

This lorry,' Parker thumbed towards the blue grey vehicle. 'How I got here I haven't got a clue. I can't even remember leaving the airfield.'

'I don't suppose you have any coffee in that truck, Percy?' asked Sherman, with a forlorn look on his face.

'You're in luck there yank, as it happens. There's a big tin of coffee beans in the back old chap.' replied Parker cordially. Sherman's face lit up, and he wasted no time in jumping up over the tailgate and searching for the coffee tin, which was stacked up next to some wooden medical boxes under an old tarpaulin.

He prised open the lid and stared down at the beautiful dark brown beans. He placed the opened tin under his nose and inhaled. The aroma almost sent him giddy. Carefully replacing the lid, he jumped down and asked Simms if he could use the kettle. The two men trotted back to refill the kettle and ignite the paraffin stove.

Evans drank the remnants of his water bottle and refilled it from the Jerry can. He checked on Macbeth and offered him his water bottle, the contents of which were poured over his head, washing away the sweat and bugs.

Evans nodded towards the lorry. 'At least we won't have to walk anymore. 'I can make up some sort of hammock in the back if you like?'

'No, I will travel in the cab. As leader of this troop, I intend to lead from the front.' Macbeth picked up Evan's water bottle, swilled some water around his mouth, and spat it out. 'Is that bloody tank still burning?' asked Macbeth. Evans got up and climbed up on the tailgate of the lorry, looking over the treeline. He could just make out the black pall of smoke still rising from the burning tank.

'I've got some binoculars in the cab, if that helps.' said Parker.

'It would indeed.' replied Evans.

Parker rummaged around in the cab and fished out the field glasses and handed them over to Evans.

'Courtesy of the Luftwaffe. One of their planes landed at our airfield by mistake and I relieved them of these fine field glasses as a memento.'

Evans examined the binoculars and noted that they were made by Carl Zeiss. He climbed up on top of the lorry cab. Once he had steadied himself, he brought the eye glasses up and adjusted the calibration. The binoculars were extremely clear and sharp. He focused in on the by now wispy smoke in the distance. As he slowly moved the glasses around, all he could see was tree tops and patches of snaking roadway dotted here and there. Evans surveyed the horizon, turning a full circle. As far as the eye could see, the horizon was covered in tree canopies and, as before, snaking sections of trackway. As he was about to finish his observations, a movement caught his eye.

Simms refilled the kettle as Sherman busied himself with grinding the precious beans. He used the inside of a helmet and the bottom of a Mills bomb as a mortar and pestle. Carefully twisting the knurled surface of the grenade to great effect. The roasted beans crumbled and powdered under his grinding action, the coffee aroma emanating from the helmet lifted their spirits.

As they waited for the water to boil, Sherman washed out a couple of mugs and set them on the ground. He carefully sprinkled the coffee powder into each mug by tapping and vibrating the side of the helmet. Simms elected to have powdered milk with his and Sherman had his black. After what seemed an age, the water boiled, and the coffee infused. The smell drifted through the air like a drug. Sherman lifted his enamel mug by the handle and cupped the other hand around the bottom of the mug in case it slipped. He brought the mug up to his nose to enjoy the almost intoxicating fragrance. Sipping the black liquid, he settled down to savour his beverage and felt almost content.

Simms, with a mug in hand, walked off down the track to see if he could find the young gunner. He was sure he would love to taste this coffee, and Simms was worried about his state of mind. He called out for him every twenty yards or so. The only reply came from the cawing crows and the hollow sounding call of the wood pigeons.

Sherman came up behind him to help, and the two men moved off into the trees. They parted by about forty yards to cover more ground, each taking it in turns to call for the youth. Sherman, stepping over a log, almost stepped into the desiccated corpse of a deer. Its bare ribs looking like a birdcage. He skirted around the log and carried on.

Simms walked on and, after calling for the boy, listened intently for any response. Repeating this search pattern, he could hear Sherman echoing the same call and listen method. As he finished his coffee, there was a call from Sherman to his left. He headed over, threading his way through the bracken and trees.

Sherman was standing in a clearing as Simms came up. A crackling, unnerving sound of heaving flies and the stench of blood pervaded the still air. This told the story before Simms even looked at the grisly sight before him. The body of the youth lay on the ground at the end of a blood trail some twenty yards long. The cadaver had had his throat ripped out, and it had ripped his lower stomach open. Sausage intestines trailed back some ten yards. His left arm was missing. Remains of bone, gristle, and tendons lay strewn nearby. Among the ferns, they found the imprints of an enormous cat, its paw pads and claws well defined. The glistening green bodied seething mass of insects, their wings catching the sun in the dappled light of the clearing, almost animated the corpse.

Simms picked up the strewn letters and other items and replaced them in Witherspoon's pack. Sherman was evidently shocked by what he had seen, his face losing most of its colour. 'Are you alright, Bill?'

'Don't get see this sort of thing at twenty thousand feet' replied Sherman.

He wanted to bury the remains there and then, but Simms insisted they move on, as the hungry animals may still be around. Checking the ground for any other letters, the two men set off. Sherman kept saying repeatedly that he didn't hear a thing. How could something like that had happened without hearing anything at all? Simms said nothing. He was thinking his own thoughts and blocking out Sherman's rant.

As the two men walked up the track towards where they thought the lorry was parked, it had disappeared. They looked at each other in disbelief. The lorry was gone.

Just as Simms's heart had started to beat faster with a surge of panic at the thought of being abandoned, Evans stepped out of the trees some yards up the track and waved them to come up.

Evans prompted them to hurry. Simms knew by the look on Evan's face that the situation was urgent. They ran the rest of the way and as Evans ushered them into the trees, Simms found Parker busy collecting fallen branches and uprooting ferns to cover the rear end of the lorry. Macbeth was hobbling about trying to help. 'What's going on?' said Simms. 'German column coming this way. Looks like a company strength. They'll be here any minute.' replied Evans.

'Fuck.' said Simms.

'Where's the boy?' asked Macbeth. Sweat beads running down his face.

'He won't be joining us.' replied Simms.

The men busied themselves finishing the final touches of camouflaging the vehicle. Evans had the onerous task of trying to cover the tracks that the lorry had made as it pulled off the road and churned up the bracken and ferns.

He moved up the track carrying a large branch with splayed leaves on the end to act as a brush. He kicked at the red-coloured soil and moved the branch from side to side, covering the tyre tracks as best as he could. Simms came and helped him lift the flattened ferns, and bolstering their coverage with other plants uprooted nearby.

They were just in time as before long they could hear the tramp of leather boots and a soft whine of an engine. They all secreted themselves under the lorry except for Evans, who crept forward to peer out of the foliage.

Just rounding a bend and leading the column came a Kublewagen. A German officer sat in the front passenger seat. He looked young and fresh faced. Evans reckoned he could put a bullet through his left eye socket, or his right one, come to that from where he was. If only he had the chance.

As the Kublewagen came abreast of Evan's position, it stopped and the young officer alighted. The soldiers marching behind came to a halt and stood at ease. Evans did a quick headcount and estimated at least seventy foot soldiers. The officer, a Hauptmann, spread out a folded map across the bonnet of the vehicle and began to study it. Evans could make out the SS insignia on his collar. Another officer, an oberleutnant, clambered out of the back seat of the Kublewagen and stretched his arms and rubbed his backside. The Hauptmann looked up from the map and walked to the side of the road, peered through his binoculars at the distant smoke. The two SS men conversed over the map before remounting the vehicle.

Simms, lying under the lorry, turned over to make himself more comfortable and inadvertently made contact with Macbeth's buttocks with his hobnailed boot. The pain shot through the little corporal like a lightning bolt. He tried very hard not to scream, but the sound that emanated was like a high-pitched squeal.

Evans froze as the Hauptmann looked straight at him. He got out of the vehicle and removed his Luger from its leather holster. He stood in the road listening. The Oberleutnant also exited the vehicle and came over to stand a few feet from Evan's position. Looking up at the SS officer through the scanty leaf covering, Evans moved his hand down and slowly retrieved his French revolver. If he was discovered as least, he could take these two fucks out first he thought.

The Oberleutnant stood almost directly over Evans, and he felt his heart pounding, waiting for the shout of discovery, waiting for the balloon to go up. Evans could smell his perfume and was surprised to see how shiny his leather boots were. At that moment, from the inner depths of the wood, came the deep throated low roar of a large cat.

The German officers exchanged some frantic words to each other and clambered back into their vehicle and, with a crunching of gears, moved off.

The formation of infantry soldiers were not quite ready and after some shouting and cajoling from the NCO's they moved off. As the procession passed by, Evans found he was looking at mere boy scouts dressed up. They reminded him of his time in the scout movement, of carefree times, of sausages cooked over an open fire and singing Ging Gang Gooley with his mates. They were smiling and laughing. Some at the rear sang with the rhyme and rhythm of their marching leather boots.

When the SS soldiers had disappeared from view, the troop cleared away the camouflage that had served them well. The lorry was disinterred and reversed back out onto the road. They thought it prudent to go in the opposite direction to the SS troops. Sherman wanted to go back and bury the remains of the boy, but was told they had to leave the area quickly. Other German units could be in the area, and now they had man-eating lions to contend with.

Evans could see that Macbeth was in a lot of pain.

'I think you could do with a little more medicine corp. There's plenty of medical   supplies in the back of the lorry.'

Macbeth was in no mood to argue he could barely stand up and the thought of being rocked around in the cab did nothing for his mood. 'Alright, just a little morphine to see how we go.' he whimpered.

Simms broke open a syrette and injected Macbeth. He soon started to relax and Evans held him as he went unconscious. A hammock was fashioned, made up from an old tarp and rope, suspended from the canopy struts.

When the last of the equipment was loaded, Macbeth was carefully lifted and laid in his suspended bed. Evans and Simms clambered in the back and the tailboard locked. Sherman sat in the cab next to Parker as the engine was fired up. Parker engaged first gear, and they were off. The lorry's six-cylinder engine growled. The gearbox whined as the lorry moved down the track, weaving its way through the trees. All the exhausted men were grateful to be riding in the lorry.

Parker drove the vehicle at a sedate pace owing to the potholed nature of the track and not wanting to roll the lumbering lorry too much. Even he was starting to feel seasick. Sherman looked out of the windscreen. 'What if we turn a bend and come face to face with the enemy, Percy?'

He looked over at Sherman and smiled. 'If there's more of them than us, we just surrender mate.'

'Have you ever been to the states Percy?'

'Can't say I have. Always wanted to go one day.'

Sherman looked over at Parker. 'I would consider it a honour if you would come over and visit me Percy. You know, when this crap is all over.'

'I would love to. Boston sounds like a great place to visit,' said Parker. He stamped on the stiff clutch pedal and changed to a lower gear. The lorry trundled on down the winding track, scattering the odd rabbits and boars that lingered in the road. In the back, Evans made a small bed among the folded sheets of tarps while Simms sat on an ammo box. Between them, swaying with the motion of the lorry, the suspended wounded corporal rocked back and fore, oblivious to the world.

After a time, the road widened a little and gave way to a glade when the lorry triggered a land mine.

The font tyre had missed the pressure trigger by a hair, but the rear tyre, being slightly wider, had caught it head on. As the explosive charge coned upwards, it ripped off the rear axle and blew the rear flatbed and all its contents to smithereens. The ammunition in the back of the lorry also ignited, bodies and debris were scattered over a large area.

Sherman was the first to recover. The cab itself had sustained minor damage, as most of the blast had dissipated at the rear. The cab door had buckled slightly and needed a good kick to open it.

His ears were ringing from the concussion as he made his way around the front of the lorry to help Parker. He pulled at the door, and after several attempts, managed to open it. Parker was dazed and slumped over the steering wheel, blood ran down his face from a gash on his forehead. Sherman lifted Parker down and carried him over to a shaded area. He cleaned up the wound and applied a bandage. Soaking a shell dressing with water, he placed it on

Parker's head to keep him cool.

Sherman sat and drank some water. His ears were returning to normal as he surveyed to scene before him. The smoke had largely dissipated and luckily the vehicle's petrol tank had not been punctured. The destroyed lorry had almost been severed in half. Boxes were everywhere. Some were intact while others were smashed open, the contents scattered over the glade. Sherman then noticed a man hanging from a tree, like a doll left there by some careless child.

A hog appeared at the edge of the glade attracted by the smell of blood. He sniffed the air and ventured further in, hunger driving his resolve. The hog disappeared from view behind the lorry cab.

Parker stood up and found an Enfield lying nearby and worked the bolt. With a snorting, grunting sound, the Hog reappeared with what looked like part of a leg in its mouth, the boot still attached.

The report of the rifle echoed around the glade as Parker dispatched the hungry hog with a clean shot through the brain. As the animal keeled over the leg and boot stuck up in the air like some grotesque art work. A gathering of crows stayed aloft.

Some of the ammunition boxes were still burning setting off the odd rifle round, like a Chinese cracker. Other boars could be heard circling around the glade, waiting for an opportunity to fest. The two men set about their task of burying these soldiers. Sherman found it was Simms's body in the tree. He was lowered down, a tarpaulin draped over him. Parker pulled out a long wooden box and prized the lid off. Inside he found a Boyes antitank rifle. The last owner had scratched his initials in the wooded butt stock.

Parker had also found a suitable box, and they set about collecting as many body parts as they could. It was impossible to tell which body part came from which man, they just guessed based on size, Evans being at least a foot taller than Macbeth. Sherman tried to recovered the leg and boot from the hog, but its jaws were so tightly clamped on the flesh, he had to cut the hogs head off. He determined that this must be

Macbeth's from the small size.

Picks and shovels were found, and they laboured, taking it turns, until three separate graves were dug.

Parker collected some wood from the broken boxes and fashioned some crosses. 'Do you know what their names were, Sherman?'

'No, I have only known them a short time, just their surnames.' said Sherman. He scraped together the last pile of earth and heaved it out of the grave.

Together they placed the one complete body and the two boxes in separate graves and backfilled the soil. Parker etched a Latin inscription on one cross and set it at the head of the central grave.

He then set a cross at the head of the other graves.

Sherman asked, 'What does *'Deus Vobiscum'* mean?'

'God be with you,' he replied. I don't know if any of them were religious or not, but it seems appropriate, even if they weren't. They seemed a good sort to me. Do you want to say a few words for them?' asked Parker.

Sherman looked at Parker. 'I guess I should. I owe so much to these guys.' He lowered his head and said.

'Now I lay me down to sleep. I pray the Lord my soul to keep. If I should die before I wake. I pray the Lord my soul to take.' Sherman took one step back and saluted.

'Sunday school. My folks sent me every week.' Sherman looked sad all of a sudden and strolled away from the graves. He started filling some water bottles from the Jerry cans that were not damaged. The two men gathered their equipment from the debris and started walking.

As they left the glade the crows and hovering hogs descended on the dead boar, and with much commotion gorged themselves.

'I hate all this walking. Do you think we could come across one of our trucks, Percy' asked Sherman.

'Its highly unlikely, I've been driving around for hours and not seen one of our lot.' Parker said, he looked at Sherman and tried to reassure the airman. 'Don't worry old chap, we'll be in Boston in no time and drinking an ice cold beer.' 'Well, Percy, when this crap is all over and you come over, I'm going to take down town to my favourite bar on Essex Street.'

The two men walked down the track, each taking a worn furrow, a green grass area between them.

'I can see now Percy, the glass, the condensation forming on the side, the gas bubbles rising to the top. They serve the best beer in Boston. You are going to love it.'

'What's the name of this bar?'

'It's called Izzy Orts.'

Printed in Great Britain
by Amazon

84982320R10108